THE TUESDAY CAFE

THE TUESDAY CAFE

DON TREMBATH

ORCA BOOK PUBLISHERS

Canadian Cataloguing in Publication Data
    Trembath, Don, 1963 –
    The Tuesday cafe

    ISBN 1-55143-074-6
    I. Title
PS8589.R392T83 1996   jC813'.54   C95-911166-2
PZ7.T71924Tu 1996

The publisher would like to acknowledge the ongoing financial support of The Canada Council, the Department of Canadian Heritage, and the British Columbia Ministry of Small Business, Tourism and Culture.

Cover design by Christine Toller
Cover painting by Ron Lightburn
Printed and bound in Canada

Orca Book Publishers
PO Box 5626, Station B
Victoria, BC Canada
V8R 6S4

Orca Book Publishers
PO Box 468
Custer, WA   USA
98240-0468

10 9 8 7 6 5

To Walker, who was not even born when I began writing this book, and can now walk and eat carrot sticks all on her own; to Riley, who I pulled in his little yellow wagon down the snowy streets to the mailbox where I mailed this manuscript, then off to the store for a treat; and to Lisa, who once said, "I know you will," when I told her I would write a book some day, and has proven to be right once again.

one

After about ten boring cases and a break that lasted almost the entire day, they called my name. Mom gave me a poke in the ribs with her elbow and said, "That's you. Get up there," in my ear. I guess she thought I'd forgotten my own name in all the excitement.

I stood up and walked to the podium at the front. Mom stood behind me.

"Harper Winslow?" said the woman at the desk. She had big brown hair and these bright red fingernails that practically blinded me when I walked into the courtroom. Her voice was deep and loud. She had a little microphone off to one side of her desk but she never used it. She didn't exactly smile much either. It was like she was saying to everyone in the courtroom, "I am going out tonight after work, and if you delinquents make me late, I am going to be very, VERY upset."

I don't know about anyone else in here, but I sure hope she gets to where she's going on time.

I nodded after she said my name, but I didn't say anything. Mom had told me to keep my mouth shut for a change, and I thought it would be a good idea to oblige her.

Mom is always offering me helpful hints about what to say and what to wear. She herself is perfect. She reads books on etiquette and *How To Raise Healthy Kids*. Naturally part of that means regular exercise, which she and my dad get every morning, but not me (I don't like exercise, it makes me sweat), which has been a sore point with them since I was about three.

My mom is five-foot-three-inches tall and weighs one hundred and four pounds. All of her friends say she is in perfect shape, but she always says, Oh no, there's room for improvement, believe me. But I'll bet you a million dollars that if you said to her, Is it me, or have you gained a pound or two since the last time I saw you? she'd pull your hair out until you were bald.

"Harper Winslow, you are charged with one count of arson causing property damage in the amount of $200. How do you wish to plea?"

"Guilty," I said. That was the one word Mom said I could say.

Then a tall, skinny guy in a light blue suit stood up at the table to my right and started reading out of this little folder he had in his hands.

"Your Honor, at approximately 10:30 on the morning of September 17, the accused, Harper Prescott Winslow of Emville, Alberta, was seen setting a fire in a garbage can in the hallway at the Emville Community High School. Witnesses say the accused set the fire by lighting a piece of paper he had torn from his binder and

2

dropping it into the trash can. Flames immediately leapt out of the basket, scaring the accused. He tipped over the trash can in his haste to exit the scene, and in doing so, he spilled burning papers all over the floor of the high school. The floors in this particular area are carpeted Your Honor and there was considerable damage done. Witnesses say that had they not been on the scene to put out the fire, the whole situation could have been much worse."

"What are you asking for?" said the judge, an older man with a wooden face that looked like it hadn't worn a smile in about fifty years. His eyes were small and jet black, and just about everyone who stood before him squirmed when he looked at them. Mom had pointed that out to me earlier.

"Your Honor, the boy's parents have already paid the necessary repair costs to the school, and have assured us that severe discipline has been handed out at home. The accused was suspended from school for one full week and warned that one more incident and he would be expelled. Taking all of this into account, Your Honor, we ask that you consider some form of community service work for the accused, and possibly some time on probation."

"This isn't the first offence, is it?" said the judge. He was looking straight at me now, and I could feel the hair on the top of my big toes starting to curl.

"No, it isn't, Your Honor."

"What were the others?"

"Mischief and theft. One charge of each."

There was silence for about a minute, then the judge

said to me, "So you decided to try to burn the school down, did you?"

Now this is where I could have said something, like, excuse me, Your Honor, but how is a kid with a book of matches going to burn down a concrete high school? But of course, I kept my mouth shut.

He continued to look at me, his face getting darker and darker.

I licked my lips and swallowed. I was starting to get a bit nervous.

"How old are you, Harper?" he asked me, breaking the silence.

"Fifteen," I said. I figured if the judge was going to ask me questions, I'd better talk.

"Pardon me?"

"Fifteen, sir," I said. My dad had told me about that sir business. He can be pretty handy with the tips, too. "When I was your age," he always says, "I called everyone older than me 'sir.' It's called *respect*." Then he goes on to tell me about all the trophies he won playing hockey, and baseball, and tennis, and about how hard he works, even today, to stay in shape. But the truth is, and Mom drives him nuts about this all the time, it's his belly that is really starting to take shape. Last year, at Christmas, she bought him a weigh scale and told him to hop on. She bet that if he was under two hundred and ten pounds, they would go to the hockey game. If he was over, they would go to the opera. They went to the opera.

"I'm six-foot-two," Dad said. "Two-ten is not overweight for six-foot-two. Look it up."

"You used to weigh one-ninety," said Mom. "You used to brag about it. One-ninety and not an ounce of fat. Remember?" Dad never said if he remembered or not.

"You're just getting old," Mom said. Dad turned fifty-eight last May. Mom is fifty-five.

The other thing is, he's starting to go bald, but I won't get into that. By the time this day is over, I might be bald myself.

"And you've been charged three times with serious crimes," said the judge.

Well, kind of yes and kind of no, sir. The mischief charge was when I was eight and hid under the bed in the spare bedroom. My parents couldn't find me so they called the police. Typical overreaction. First I get no attention at all; then I have Emville's finest (which ain't so hot, I can tell you) combing the bushes looking for me.

It was the sergeant who found me.

"Anybody look under the beds?" I heard him say, approaching the door to the room I was in. He didn't wait for an answer. At least, I didn't hear one. He just bent down and flipped up the covers, and there I was, flashlight in hand, reading a comic book.

"Well, well," the sergeant said. "We've been looking for you."

They charged me with mischief.

"We were terrified," my mother had said when it was all over, as she searched madly in her purse for the phone number of a person she had to call before her Chamber of Commerce meeting.

"If you ever pull something like this again ... ," said

my dad, who had hurried straight home after his last appointment to take part in the search.

The theft charge was even dumber, mainly because I didn't steal anything. It happened last year. I was in this little store, Redi-Mart, to be precise, buying a slush, when all of a sudden the owner, this little Chinese guy that no one can understand, not even his own wife, and she's Chinese, locks the doors and starts calling everybody a bunch of crooks.

Somebody finally gets the guy calmed down, and he says that somebody had swiped the wallet out of his wife's purse. I guess her purse had been at the back of the store or something, near the pop. Why anyone would leave an open purse at the back of a convenience store is beyond me, but that apparently didn't matter.

We were all thieves until somebody fessed up to the crime. Some grade tens who didn't want to be late for phys. ed. looked around and saw me and told me to confess. One of them knew my name.

"Hey, Winslow," he said. I didn't know who he was. Some guy with red hair and a big set of knuckles he held up under my nose. "You steal this lady's wallet?"

Now you tell me what I would be doing standing around waiting for a cream soda slush if I had swiped this lady's wallet. And even if I had swiped it, where did I put it? It wasn't on me. It wasn't anywhere. No one could find the stupid thing.

"Maybe you ran out and hid it somewhere and came back," said the guy with his knuckles under my nose, after I raised the question with him.

All I could do was hope he wasn't contagious.

"Hey, is that the doctor's kid?" said somebody else.

"Yeah, it is," said Knuckles.

"The spoiled doctor's kid stealing money from an innocent immigrant," said The Somebody Else, who I am sure did not know what an immigrant was. "I should pop you in the mouth, you little twerp. Come on. Give her back her wallet."

The threat of violence scared someone into calling the RCMP, and within the hour a car came screeching up to the store, lights flashing, and I was soon led away.

They charged me with theft, even though they never found anything on me. A day later the Chinese lady phoned the police and told them she had found her wallet at the bank, where she had left it by mistake while making a deposit.

I did not have to go to court, but apparently someone forgot to take the charge off my record.

"Actually two, sir," I said to the judge. "The theft charge was dropped. It was a mistake."

"So that makes it okay then?" said the judge. He was really starting to get upset.

"I was just — "

"Don't you *just anything* in this courtroom, young man!" He was hot now. He slammed his gavel down so hard the glass of water he had on his desk tipped on its side and the water ran over the edge.

"Now look what you've done!" he cried, leaping to his feet. "Carolyn!" he bellowed to the woman sitting at the desk below him, who suddenly looked very much alive. "Get me a towel. No, *you*!" he roared, pointing a finger at me as if it was a gun. "*You* get a towel and you clean this mess up! Get moving!"

I stood frozen for a second, then somebody opened a door at the side of the courtroom and flipped the lady named Carolyn a towel. She passed it to me. The look on her face said that she had reached her very, VERY upset stage. I went to where the judge was standing and mopped up the water. He was fuming.

"Down there!" he said, pointing to a few drops on the floor.

When I was finished, I walked back to the podium and handed the towel to my mom.

"You hang on to it!" roared the judge again. "You've passed on enough to your parents already!"

His lips were shaking, he was so mad.

"I happen to know your mother and father, young man," he said, after taking a few deep breaths. You could tell he was trying to keep from losing it again. "I know them very well in fact. I know they have committed their very lives to the betterment of this town, and that a lot of people have benefitted enormously from their generosity. And you've just gone and tried to *burn it all down*!" Ka-boom! went the gavel again. I jumped about a foot in the air. "You should be *ashamed of yourself, Harper Winslow*! You should be embarrassed by your behavior. Embarrassed by what you've done. Instead I don't sense a bit of remorse in you. That whole school could be a pile of ashes right now and I don't think you'd care, would you? *Would you?*"

"Yes, I would care, sir," I said. I wasn't kidding either. I was scared to death.

"What would you care about?" He snapped. I was really under interrogation now.

"I would care if my school burned down. I didn't want to burn it down. I was just mad."

"What were you mad about?"

"I had to clean the locker room again for no reason and I didn't like it."

"Why didn't you like it?"

"Because I always have to do it."

"So you started a fire."

"Yes. I guess I did."

"A fire that could have burned down the entire school. The entire school that was full of students and teachers at the time."

"Well, I really don't see how that little fire could have burned down the entire school, but — "

" — Oh, you don't?"

"Not really. No."

"And what makes you an expert on fires?"

"I'm not an expert, sir."

"Oh, you're not? But you still don't think there was any risk there?"

"Well, maybe there was."

"There either was or there wasn't. Which is it?"

"I don't know, sir."

"You don't know?"

"No, I don't."

"That's the most intelligent thing I've heard you say.

Of course, you don't know. How could you know? How could I have known I was going to spill water on myself today? How can someone know when they're going to get hit by a car? They don't know, that's how. That's why we discourage people from doing stupid things like setting fires in trash cans in the middle of a school. Because accidents can happen and neither you nor I nor anyone else can prevent them."

He took a breather and leaned back in his chair, but his eyes never left me.

"How are you doing at school, Harper?" he said.

"Not so hot, Your Honor," I said.

"Do you have many friends?"

"Not really."

"How are your grades?"

"Cs mostly. A few Ds."

"Do you like sports?"

"No."

"I beg your pardon?"

"No, sir."

"Do you have a girlfriend?"

"No, sir."

"What kind of interests do you have? What do you do when you're not in school?"

I couldn't think of anything. I was starting to feel pretty lousy.

"Your Honor?" said my mother behind me. "Can I say something?"

"Of course, Mrs. Winslow. Step forward, please." All of a sudden he was Mr. Kindness.

So Mom stepped forward. The heels on her shoes went click, click on the floor, and she smoothed her hair with her fingers. She just got a new hairdo — short, blunt, and sassy, she likes to call it — and she checks to see what she looks like wherever we go. She used to take me with her whenever she went to have her hair done, which seemed like every second day, but ever since I said, after she asked me what I thought she should do, "Just shave the stupid thing," and made the hairdresser laugh, she has left me at home. I was grounded for that little comment. In hindsight, calling her head a "stupid thing" was not a brilliant idea.

"Your Honor, Harper really enjoys reading. He loves books. And he has tried writing before, but he has always stopped before he finishes what he's doing."

"Thank you, Mrs. Winslow," said the judge.

Mom stepped back.

"So you fancy writing, do you?" he said, looking back at me. I shrugged my shoulders, but he didn't notice.

"Well then, here is your sentence. You will do forty hours of community service work at your school. I will arrange with one of your counsellors to keep track of your work.

"And you will submit to me within one month of today a two thousand word essay entitled, "How I Plan To Turn My Life Around." It will be type-written, double-spaced, and if it is not in on time, or if it does not reflect any serious thought on your behalf, then I will come down on you like a prairie rainstorm, only I won't let up.

"Do you understand your sentence?"

"Yes, I do, sir," I said. I didn't really, but I didn't think now would be the time to ask for clarification.

"You can obtain help if you want, but you will be in big trouble if I find out someone else had a direct hand in the actual writing, and so will the person who helps you. Is that understood?"

"Yes, sir."

"I'm giving you a break here, Harper. I hope you realize that. It is because of your parents. They are two wonderful people, and I have had the pleasure of meeting your older brother and sister and I have found them to be wonderful too, and I have no reason to believe you can't work out to be the same."

"Thank you, sir," I said. But I didn't really mean it.

"That will be all. Next case please, Carolyn."

Carolyn immediately bellowed out another name, and then she looked at me as if to say, Move it! So I did.

Mom and I left the courtroom together. When we got to the car she started in again about how lucky I was that my father is so well connected, and how she hoped to hell that I'd learned my lesson.

She dropped me off at home and told me there were leftovers in the fridge for supper. She wouldn't be home and neither would Dad.

I went inside and flopped on the couch. I was still feeling pretty lousy. Maybe I am lucky to have the kind of family I do, but I sure don't feel it.

I didn't bother eating anything for supper. I just hung around and then went to bed. I didn't even think about the stupid essay.

two

A couple of days later a big story ran in the *Emville Eyeopener* about the kid who set a fire in the new high school. Teachers who hadn't even known there was a fire were quoted as saying they were scared to death, and the chairman of the school board suggested immediate expulsion would have been a more suitable punishment.

"This school is the heart and soul of the community," he said in the paper. "And already we have people trying to destroy it. It makes me sick."

Now I was a cancer.

My name was withheld from the press, in accordance with the Young Offenders' Act, which also came under attack, but just about everyone in town knew who the story was about.

I got threatened a few times. It seems the flick of my Bic lighter ignited the civic pride in every tough who ever hung out at the schoolyard with a smoke hanging from his mouth. I was pushed and shoved and Darren Talbot put me in a headlock.

Mr. Jorgenson, the phys. ed. teacher who started the whole thing by telling me to clean out the locker room for the fourth time in two weeks, even though it is supposed to be a job that everyone gets a turn at, was standing right there when Tony Phillips and Trevor Connors knocked my books out of my hands, sending paper all over the place, but he never said anything.

It was open season on me, basically, and everybody was taking a shot.

Dad came out of the whole thing smelling like a rose, of course. People who didn't even have an appointment stopped by the clinic to say how sorry they felt for him and Judy, my mom, and how they wished everything would get turned around.

The mayor phoned to have a talk with him. Dad is a town councillor, so he and the mayor are good friends. They talked for about an hour.

The same thing happened with Mom. She got hugs from people in the grocery store and anyone who walked into her boutique smiled and wished her well.

It was like there had been a death in the family.

If Dad had had his way, there would have been, but Mom managed to cool him down. She said to him, "Look, honey, his name wasn't in the paper. No one outside town will ever know, and besides, look at the support you're getting."

He liked hearing that. Dad is thinking about taking a stab at provincial politics one year, so he is very concerned about his image, not that he wasn't before.

After Mom talked he threw back the rest of his scotch

and nodded his head, meaning okay, fine, next topic, please.

"Did I tell you what Rowland wants him to do?" Mom continued. They were talking in the living room. I was sitting at the top of the stairs, supposedly thinking about my assignment, but really listening to them.

"Good old Rollie," said Dad, shaking his head, then leaning back against the couch. "Doing us a big favor. Make the boy write an essay. Just what he needs."

"I think it's a terrific idea," said Mom. "I think it is just what he needs. Something to get him thinking about his life."

"How is he ever going to put an essay like that together?" said Dad, his confidence in me coming through loud and clear.

Dad believes in confidence. He has a big picture of himself in his office at home, shaking hands with the mayor. Dad had just been elected as one of the town councillors. He is pretty serious looking most of the time, but in this picture, he has a big smile on his face. He wasn't wearing glasses then, and his hair was still more black than gray.

"That is a picture of a confident man," he always tells me. "I want to see you in a picture like that, someday."

"Okay," I always say, as if it was just a matter of standing in front of a camera and looking confident.

"It's not simply a matter of standing in front of a camera and looking confident," he always says. "Confidence is something that goes from the inside out."

My dad has a deep, strong voice, and there are lots

of times when I think his favorite pastime in the world is to hear himself talk, especially when it comes to stuff like this.

"I've signed him up with a writing group," said Mom. She is so efficient. Then I did a double take. *A writing group? What writing group? What is a writing group?* "It's called The Tuesday Cafe. It's a writing class. They meet in the city every Tuesday night at some school or something. Or a cafe, I guess."

"How'd you hear about it?"

"There was an ad for it in the yellow pages. I phoned and left a message on their machine. I saw it quite by mistake actually."

"What's the message say?"

"It says the next session starts this Tuesday and to be there at seven o'clock."

"That's it?"

"No. It went on about something-or-other. Phyllis Charmichael walked in with her daughter's wedding dress, so I wasn't really listening."

"What's wrong with Phyllis Charmichael's daughter's wedding dress this time?"

"It's not big enough."

Dad started to laugh. "They better check the doors of the church. See if they're big enough."

"Ben!" said Mom, but she was laughing, too.

Dad can be pretty funny sometimes, when he's not busy being Dr. Benjamin Winslow, or Councillor Benjamin Winslow, or Friend-Of-All-The-People Benjamin Winslow.

"I suppose that means another ride to the city," he said, rubbing his eyes. The city he's talking about is Edmonton. It's about a forty-kilometer drive, one way.

"I can take him," said Mom. "I'll make Tuesday my shopping night."

She means for material for the dresses she makes. Mom sews dresses and pant suits and sells them in the store she runs. She does her own designs and everything. She's pretty good, too, I guess. She put my dad through med school doing it.

My dad has been a doctor for thirty-two years. He graduated the same year my brother William was born.

Dad always tells the story of when he and my mom were at the big graduation banquet for all of these med students, and right in the middle of it my mom starts going into labor, and Dad, number four in the entire graduating class, faints face down in his dessert.

My sister Clarissa was born a year later.

Dad says he used to take my brother and sister with him on his house calls, so my mom could catch up on either her sleeping or her sewing, whichever she chose. He used to say that when she caught up on her sleeping, she would want to sew when the kids went to bed, but if she caught up on her sewing, she'd "be frisky and want to catch up with me. So whenever I'd come home and see the light on in her sewing room, I'd slip the kids a nickel apiece and tell them to run up to bed."

People always laugh when he tells those stories. Even people he's known for twenty years, or longer, some of them.

He never tells any stories about me, though. He just says, "Harper, by the time you came along, all the good stories were used up already." You gotta believe him, too.

My brother moved out of the house to go to university when I was two and my sister followed the day after my fourth birthday. I remember my mom crying all over the place at my birthday party and William telling me to knock it off when I asked why there was no money in the cake.

Dad heard us and slapped a quarter down in front of me and told me to stop being so insensitive. I didn't even know what the word meant.

" — hope this doesn't take up a lot of your time. This is Harper's mess and he should have to clean it up himself," Dad was saying. I'd lost track of them for a minute.

"It won't," said Mom. "It can't. I have all the gowns for the Charmichael wedding party to do, and the Johnson's after that. I don't have a lot of time to give up."

"Good," said Dad. Then he got off the couch. He had a meeting to go to. The Hospital Board or something. It was Thursday so my mom would be home until 7:30, then she would go to the seniors' home with a shawl or a blanket she had made on the weekend and give it away at the bingo.

Neither of them had spoken to me much since my day in court. Dad said he was too upset to even talk about it, but that didn't stop him from going on and on whenever anyone phoned or came by the door. And Mom told me this morning that she had already said everything she had to say about it, but obviously she hasn't, because how am I ever going to find out about this Tuesday Cafe thing? Whatever that is.

Dad left and Mom ran the dishwasher and did a few things in the basement. My brother and sister are coming over on the weekend and Mom always gets the toys ready for their kids. Then she put on her coat and boots and stepped out the door.

Nobody even says good-bye anymore.

three

I went and met Ms. Davis today. She's the school counsellor. I have been ordered to spend two hours a week
with her until the end of the year. She told me Mondays
and Wednesdays were fine for her, which meant they
were fine for me, too, so we set up our appointments for
Monday and Wednesday mornings. Today is Monday.

I have never been in her office before, but I know
who Ms. Davis is. She's always coming to the classrooms and telling everybody about the programs she's
offering and what her job is. She is a Guidance Counsellor. She helps to guide people like me through the
"sometimes difficult years of adolescence and high
school" — these are her exact words.

She is always smiling and she always says hi when
she passes me in the hallway, even though, like I said, I
have never really met her before. I doubt if she even
knew my name.

She has long auburn hair that never looks the same
because she's always braiding it or wearing it up or
down. She wears glasses, but she looks good in them,

unlike every other person in the school who wears glasses. Or, most of them, anyway.

She buys her clothes at my mom's store, so Mom is naturally crazy about her. "That Sally Davis, she is such a lovely girl. And what a figure. I would die for that figure. She can walk into the store and wear just about anything. I want her to model but she wants nothing to do with it.

"Now she would be a good teacher for you, Harper."

"She's not a teacher," I always say. She is not anything like a teacher. She's funny and nice and cares about people.

The first thing she did after I sat down was ask me about the fire I started. She wanted to know why I started it, so I told her the bit about cleaning out the locker room again, then she said, "No. I want the real reason."

I didn't say anything for about a minute. I just stared at her. Then I started balling my eyes out. I was crying and crying. I've never done that before in my life, not even in front of my mom, and there I was crying like crazy in front of this woman I didn't even know.

Then she asked me a real stupid question. She said, "Who are you crying for, Harper?"

It was so stupid I didn't even know the answer to it, so I just kept on crying. Then she said again, "Who are all the tears for, Harper?"

She was talking real softly and was leaning towards me in her chair. I could smell her perfume.

"My dog," I said. I was just being smart. I don't even have a dog. My parents wouldn't let me get one.

"What's your dog's name?" she said.

"Arnie," I said. I didn't even know what I was talking about.

"What kind of dog is Arnie?"

"A boxer," I said, between sniffs. I was starting to settle down.

"What does he look like?"

"He's about this high," I said, putting my hand about a foot above the floor. "And he's black and white, with these two big black patches over both his eyes."

"What do you and Arnie like to do together?" she said.

Boy, I was really getting into it now.

"We like the same books," I said. "We read a lot. He likes the same potato chips I do. He's a bit of a pig though, so we can't eat them in the living room. We have to go upstairs to my room and eat them there if we want to watch TV."

"What kind of books do you read?"

"Westerns mostly. Detective stuff. My brother left a whole bunch of books in the basement that I go through all the time. I like Mickey Spillane. Arnie likes Zane Grey and Louis L'Amour cause there's usually a picture of a horse on the cover."

"Those are adult books, are they not?"

"I don't know. I don't have a problem understanding them or anything."

She started to laugh a bit when I said that. It made me feel good to make her laugh, even though I had no idea what was so funny.

22

She didn't say anything for a minute, then she said, "Did something happen to Arnie, Harper?"

I could feel my chin start to wiggle and pretty soon the old tears were running down my cheeks again. It was all so stupid. There I was crying about a dog that didn't even exist and talking to this person who was supposed to be helping me, even though I don't need any help.

Some help she was even if I did. I go into her office feeling fine and ten minutes later I'm a babbling moron. Gee thanks, doc. Next time I think I'll take two aspirins and hop into bed.

"Tell me what happened to Arnie," she said again.

I sniffed and shook my head. What was I supposed to tell her? That Arnie is a figment of my imagination? She'd send me to the nuthouse.

"Do you and Arnie still read together?"

I nodded. I didn't know what I was saying anymore.

"Was Arnie hurt or anything?"

"No," I said.

"So why were you crying for Arnie?"

I shrugged my shoulders.

"What makes you think you were crying for Arnie?"

I shrugged my shoulders again. I was looking down at the floor during all of this. I couldn't look her in the eye.

"Suppose I say I think those tears were for you, what would you say to that?"

"Maybe they were," I said. I barely mumbled it, actually. I didn't feel much like talking, or thinking, for that matter.

She was silent for a minute, then she said, "I know you don't have a dog, Harper."

She floored me when she said that. She knew all along and she never said anything. I looked up at her and she was staring right at me with this sympathetic look on her face. I had never noticed before, but she has big, deep brown eyes that she was practically hypnotizing me with.

"I talked to your parents before you came here today. They mentioned something about how you've always wanted a dog, but they didn't think you were responsible enough for one. Now they think you've just proved them right. Is that right, Harper? Are you not responsible enough to take care of a dog like Arnie?"

I was silent for a minute, then I said, "If my mom and dad were so responsible, I wouldn't even be here."

Then I got up and left.

four

My big night is finally here. The Tuesday Cafe awaits my arrival. Oh boy, am I thrilled about this.

Mom makes it out like I'm going to be sitting at some outdoor bistro in Paris with all of these writers I've never heard of, drinking cognac, whatever that is. I think it's a bit cold to be sitting outside, thank you very much.

She said to me this morning, "Harper, I am so excited for you. I just know something good is going to come of this."

I'm excited, too, Mom. As soon as you drop me off, I'm going to hop a bus to Edmonton Center and check out the arcade.

On our way downtown, Mom has me read the address to her about a million times before we find the place.

She kept saying, "There are no cafes around here. There're no bistros or coffee shops around here."

The address we were looking for is an old two-story building with one light on in an office upstairs, and another light by the front door.

Mom pulled up to the curb and parked the car. Then she turned the engine off.

"What are you doing?" I said.

"I'm going up there with you. We have to register. We'll probably have to pay for something. Come on. Get your mitts and get moving."

"What if I don't want you to come up with me?" I said. It's my writing class, isn't it? I should have some say in whether she comes up with me or not.

She gave me one of those "Get serious, Harper" looks and stepped out of the car. So much for the arcade.

We went up the two flights of stairs, then turned the corner and saw a door with a piece of paper taped to it. On the paper were the words, in big, bold black letters, "THE TUESDAY CAFE WRITING CLASS. COME IN."

Mom smiled and gave me a little nudge. I thought to myself that if I ran now, I could probably catch a bus and be well on my way to Calgary before she got her shopping done, and be down in Montana or somewhere by the time Dad got home from his councillors' meeting.

"Come on, Harper. Knock on the door," she said.

"It says come in."

"Then go in," she said.

I turned the doorknob and pushed open the door. The sound of shrill chimes rang out, making me wince. Why do people invite you into their office, then have these chimes that could make a dog go deaf hooked up to the door? Why don't they just make you knock?

We stood in the little lobby. There was a desk with a computer on it in front of us. To the right was a little

26

boardroom. To the left was a room with a bunch of tables and chairs. There was carpeting everywhere and all of these posters on the walls about reading and writing.

There was nothing cafe-ish about the place, and I was about to make a suggestion to Mom that we'd been had, when this young guy walked out from the other room. He seemed surprised to see us.

"Oh, hi," he said.

"Hello," said Mom. I got the feeling she still thought this place was going to be great for me. Somehow. "I'm Judy Winslow. This is my son, Harper."

We all shook hands. I managed a smile. He told us his name is Josh Simpson.

He did not look like a writing teacher. He was tall and had big, wide shoulders and hands that could pick up a basketball. He had a brushcut. He looked like an athlete to me, maybe a swimmer or a high jumper, and Mom, who always gives people the once-over when she sees them for the first time, gave him about three once-overs, which means she had probably designed his entire wardrobe for the upcoming year and, at some point during my stay here, would suggest something like an olive V-neck sweater and simple white T-shirt to go with his blue jeans. He was about thirty years old, so she would undoubtedly recommend loafers over the running shoes he was wearing. I prefer the running shoes myself.

He seemed nice enough, but he was obviously confused, and that made me wonder. What could be so confusing about this? He ran a writing course. Mom signed me up for his writing course. Mom and I showed

27

up at his writing course on the night he told us to. What's the problem?

"You're here for the … " he said. He let us finish the sentence for him.

"The writing course," said Mom. "The Tuesday Cafe, I believe it's called." She said it like one of those faggy French waiters you see on TV. *The Tuesday Cafe, monsieur? Ah Oui. An excellent choice! Tres bon!*

"You are?" he said. He was very surprised.

"Didn't you get my message?" said Mom. "I phoned here last week. Last Thursday, to be precise."

Mom can be very precise.

"Oh. Okay," said Josh. "No, I didn't get your message. The janitor here turns off the machine by accident sometimes when he's cleaning. He's very enthusiastic. But that's alright, so long as you know what we're about."

"You teach writing, isn't that correct?" said Mom. She is really one of the few people I know who uses the word "correct" in conversation.

"That's right. We teach writing. Well, we don't really teach it. I don't think you can do that. But this is where you come if you want to write."

Mom looked relieved. For a second there, I think she was starting to have the same doubts I was.

"Harper here has to write an essay as part of his punishment for starting a fire at the high school in Emville," she said.

I looked at her and shook my head. The lady wears wigs, she is so worried about her own image, but with me, forget it. Everything is right out in the open. Even with a complete stranger who is still looking at us like we'd gotten off at the wrong stop.

"Oh really?" said Josh. He looked at me and smiled. His smile made me feel good, for some reason. It wasn't a big, goofy grin or anything like that. It was a real smile. Sort of a caring smile, like the way Ms. Davis always looks at me. "Well, the furnace works just fine here, so leave your matches at home."

That made me laugh a little bit. Mom didn't like it though.

"It's very serious. He could have burned down the whole school. He has to perform forty hours of community service work and write a two-thousand-word essay on how he's going to turn his life around. Don't you, Harper. You can speak, you know."

She gets like this when she's put off. She starts to pick at me, even though it's not really me she's mad at. She's mad at Josh because he didn't call me a bad boy for starting the fire.

I was starting to like this guy myself.

"Okay, well, I hope we can help you out, but in the meantime, here it is," he said, waving his arm towards the rooms behind him. "This is the Tuesday Cafe. There's coffee in the back room there, although I doubt you drink coffee. I think we have some pop in the fridge. If not, somebody usually brings some. You can get some from them. I can give you pens and paper and everything. We meet in there (he points to the room with the tables and chairs). If you want to write your essay, you can. I don't think we've ever had anybody write an essay here before, but that's okay. There's always a first time."

"What do you usually write?" asked Mom. Her manner was noticeably cooler now.

"Stories. Poems. We've done a play once, but it kind of fell apart. We have a little newspaper we do once a month. It's called *The Popsicle Journal*. You can write in that if you want."

He said the last part looking at me.

"And what exactly is *The Popsicle Journal* about?" said Mom.

"Whatever they want it to be," said Josh. "Last time out it was about dogs. The time before that they wrote about movie stars, or was it "Star Trek"? I can't remember."

Mom started to look skeptical, like she was really starting to think twice about the place, but I was starting to warm up to it a bit, so I looked at my watch and said, "Hey, Mom, if you wanna get all that shopping done before nine, you better leave now."

She turned and gave me a look.

"This is a switch," she said.

I gave her a smile. "If I start writing now, I can get an extra twenty minutes in before the others arrive," I said.

She looked like she could put cyanide in my soup and not lose a minute's sleep over it.

"Well, I do hope you plan on doing more with my son than writing about dogs in some journal," she said.

Way to get on his good side, Mom.

"This is a writing class not a day care, Mrs. Winslow. Your son can write about whatever he wants and he'll get all the assistance he needs. And if he doesn't like it, or you don't think it's enough, you can always go home," said Josh.

My ears just about fell off my head. I looked at my mom. She looked like *she'd* just had a big bowl of cyanide soup.

When was the last time someone talked like that to her? Try never and you'd be in the ballpark.

"Alright then," she said, pulling on her gloves. It looked like her fingers were going to come through the other end she was yanking on them so hard. "Harper, you heard the man. This isn't a day care. You're here to work. Let's see some results. Judge Tucksbury is not a man to keep waiting.

"I'll meet you downstairs at nine o'clock."

And with that, she finally left.

I turned to say something to Josh, but he was already in the other room moving some tables and chairs around. I went and asked him if he needed a hand. He said no, so I went back and sat in the lobby.

I felt comfortable already and I had a big smile on my face thinking about the way he had talked to my mom. Then the phone rang. Josh told me to leave it. After the third ring, the answering machine kicked on.

"Hello and welcome to the Tuesday Cafe Writing Class. Our next session begins Tuesday, November 8 and will run from 7:00 to 9:00 PM for ten weeks. Please leave your name and phone number if you would like to register.

"If you are calling for information, the Tuesday Cafe is a writing class geared towards adults with special needs, learning disabilities, or those wanting to improve their literacy skills.

"Should you have any questions, please call this number on Tuesday or Thursday afternoon and ask for Josh Simpson. Thank you for calling. Bye."

The machine clicked and whirred and recorded a message from someone named Debra who said she'd be late for tonight's class.

Now I know what my mother missed when Phyllis Charmichael walked in with her daughter's wedding dress, and why Josh was so surprised to see us.

Suddenly, I was not feeling so comfortable.

five

The first person to arrive was a guy who seemed to be about twenty-five or so. He had dark brown hair cut too short on the sides and with a bit too much goop in it. It looked like his hair hadn't seen a comb or brush in weeks — like maybe he just ran his hand from one side of his head to the other. He wore thick glasses that had little pieces of surgical tape at the corners to hold the frames together and his blue jeans had four-inch cuffs. He was a little taller and heavier than me, but the parka he was wearing could have fit my dad, who is about twice the size of both of us.

"Hey, Billy," said Josh, who came to greet the guy at the door. "How goes?"

"I lost my mitt," said Billy. His voice was high and soft, like a little kid's. His glasses were fogging over from going from the cold outside to the heat inside, so he was looking around as best he could, trying to see where Josh was standing. "I only have one now."

It was a purple mitt. His parka was army green. The toque sticking out of his pocket was bright red. Mom would have had a heart attack.

"Where'd you lose it?" said Josh.

Billy's unprotected hand was almost white it was so cold. He was shaking it in the air as if he wanted to get it off his arm, but he seemed even more concerned with his glasses. He took them off with his good hand and breathed on them to remove the fog, but his other hand was too cold to wipe them, so he rubbed them against the arm of his coat and put them back on.

"There. That's better. I lost it on the bus," he said.

"Just now?" said Josh. "How can your hand get so cold on a bus?"

"No. Not now," said Billy, shaking his head. He was very dramatic. He shook his head as if he wanted to get rid of that too. "Last year. I lost it last year coming home from the Space Sciences Center. We were playing football with it and someone threw it in this lady's bag and she walked off with it."

"Why didn't you get it back?" said Josh.

"What was I gonna say?" said Billy. "Gimme back my football? Forget it. It's hers. She can have it. It didn't work anyway. There was no thumb in it."

"You had a mitt that didn't have a thumb on it?" said Josh.

"My dog ripped it off. I used to hide my mitts in the fridge so my dog wouldn't rip them apart."

"What do you do now?" said Josh.

"He goes after my slippers now. I used to have two pairs of slippers, now they're all little pieces. I don't wear slippers anymore. I just wear my socks."

Josh stood shaking his head for a moment with a look on his face that seemed to say, Only you could come up with a story like that, Billy. Then he said, "Well come on in and take off your coat and warm up. Have a coffee. You're making me cold standing there."

As Billy took off his parka, a woman walked in and gave him a shove from behind. She was very short, not even five feet tall, I would say, and was stoutly built. Her hair was a large oval of tight little brown curls, and she had small, round-framed glasses. She looked at Josh and smiled and held her index finger over her mouth the way you do when you want someone to be quiet.

"Who did that?" said Billy, turning around. "Patty!"

She laughed. "Got you again," she said. Then she punched him on the arm.

"Ouch!" said Billy. He was being dramatic again, but this time with a smile on his face.

"I got you again, didn't I?" said Patty. She was excited. She was laughing and rocking from foot-to-foot. She couldn't stand still.

"See if I take you to the movies again," said Billy. He was still rubbing his arm where she punched him.

"You guys, this is Harper," said Josh. They looked at me but didn't say anything. Billy stopped rubbing his arm. Patty stopped smiling. "Harper, this is Billy and Patty."

I nodded and said hi.

"Who are you?" said Patty. Her face fell into a frown.

"I'm here for the writing class," I said.

She continued to look at me, reminding me of a teacher I had in grade five. She was one of those

no-nonsense teachers who used to make me spell three
words at the front of the class every morning because
my spelling, as she put it, "was awful." I did not like
that teacher.

"What for?" said Patty.

"What for? Because I want to improve my writing."
I didn't think I had to tell her about the fire and everything. She wasn't really a teacher.

She said nothing for a moment, but as we stood opposite each other, she did a quick scan of me, from head
to toe, the way Mom does whenever she meets someone. Then she said, "I don't like your shirt."

"My shirt?" I said. What was so wrong with my shirt?
It was a simple blue sweatshirt. "My mom bought me
this shirt. What's wrong with it?"

"I don't like the color."

"Oh." I looked at the color. It was mid-blue. Not
dark blue or navy blue, but not baby blue either. It was
my favorite color.

"I don't mind it," said Billy. He was nodding his
head up and down, and his forehead was burrowed, as if
he had given the matter some serious thought, and had
finally reached a conclusion. "I like the color. It's better
than green."

"I like green," said Patty, directing her eyes at Billy.
But her glare was much less severe when she looked at
him.

"Green is too green," said Billy. Now he was wrin-
kling his nose and shaking his head from side to side. "I
don't know. I don't like it. Green reminds me of golf and

don't like golf. I played it once and lost all my clubs."

"How did you do that?" I said. I wasn't sure if it was my place to ask questions or not, and usually I am pretty quiet in places like school and classrooms, but how someone could lose a set of golf clubs was something I had to know.

"I put them down to look for a ball I hit in the bush, and I forgot where I put them. I never found them again."

"Did you find the ball?" I said.

"Oh yeah. I always find lost golf balls. Even when I'm not looking for them I find them."

We stood silent for a moment after that, then Josh, who had left to get spare notepads and pens from the supply room, returned and said, "Okay, Patty, Billy, and Harper, why don't you go sit down?"

I thought that was a great idea. We all walked into the room with the tables and chairs. Billy went straight to a chair on the far side of the classroom by the window and sat down. I took a seat by the door. Patty, who took a minute to hang her coat, walked up to my desk a few moments later and stood beside me.

"Hi," I said, trying to be friendly. Maybe she was going to try again.

"You're in my seat," she said.

I got up in about half-a-second and moved to another table. Then I looked back at her and said, "Sorry about that. I didn't know."

"Now you do," she said, sitting down. Then she pulled a bright green scribbler from her book bag, and a pointy-sharp pencil, and a box of orange juice, and looked at me again. I looked away, this time for good.

A few minutes later two more people arrived. I could hear them talking and laughing with Josh in the lobby. When they walked into the room we were in, Josh said, "Harper, this is Lou and Del. They are not a couple. They just walked in together. Purely coincidence."

The woman, Del, laughed. "No, we're not a couple," she said. Then she added, "What an unusual first name. Harper. What is that, Scottish?"

I shrugged my shoulders. I have no idea what kind of a name Harper is.

Del was a big woman — tall and heavy — with short, wavy brown hair and a pair of glasses hanging on a string around her neck. Even her hands were big, like my dad's hands. She reminded me of the woman at the courthouse for a minute, but her face, when she got up close, was very bright and friendly. I liked her voice, too. It was a high voice, but happy, not whining.

"Your mother's maiden name, right?" she said.

I nodded. "I thought so. Well, hello." She came over and shook my hand. Her hand was warm and soft. She reminded me of the kind of mother you see on TV all the time. The kind all the kids go to when they have a problem. She looked to be about fifty, so she probably was a mother.

She said hi to the others, then took a seat at the front of the class.

Lou didn't say anything to anyone. He walked over to a seat near Billy and sat down. I didn't mind for one second that he was sitting on the opposite side of the room from me. He was very scary looking. He had long, shaggy, gray hair that stuck out beneath an old, dirty green baseball cap. His face was hard and unsmiling. He stood about six-foot-three and had a pot belly that was the size of Patty. His hands were rough and calloused. He was probably about Del's age, or a little older.

I laughed to myself when I thought of what Josh had said about the two of them not being a couple. I think I would have figured that one out on my own.

Del chatted with Billy for a few minutes about the weather and Lou got up to get himself a cup of coffee. He asked if anyone else wanted one. His voice was surprisingly soft for such a big man, and when I looked at him to say no, he nodded and touched the peak of his cap, as if to say hello. Now I wasn't so sure if he was hard and tough or not.

He grimaced as he walked and rubbed the lower part of his back with one of his hands as he went through the door.

About five minutes later we were joined by two more women. One was thin and pale. She looked almost sick, in fact. She had black hair and dark, dark eyes. She smiled when she saw me. Her name was Susan. I smiled and told her my name was Harper.

"Hi, Hooper," she said. She sat at the table a few over from mine and waved to Del and said hi to Billy and Patty.

"You got your hair done," she said to Patty. "I like it."

I turned and looked at Patty. She was patting her hair and smiling.

"I got a permanent," she said.

"Hey, I just thought of something," said Billy. "Why do they call it a 'permanent' when you have to keep getting one all the time? That doesn't make sense. You should be able to get one and wear it for the rest of your life."

"Good question," said Del.

"I'm gonna write that down," said Billy. "I'm gonna figure that out one day."

"I like it," said Susan again, still looking at Patty.

The other woman sat in the chair right beside mine. She had short brown hair, thick glasses, and the wildest loudest jacket in the world. It was made up of dozens of colors and patterns and shapes, all just thrown together. She was eating a rice cake.

"I can't eat bread," she said, after she saw me looking at the food in her hand. "I'll get a ratch." She dropped the book bag that hung from her shoulder to the floor and looked straight at me, as if she was studying my face.

"Mind if I look at you for a minute?" she said.

I felt a little uncomfortable, but I didn't say anything. Something told me that even if I said, Yes, I do mind if you look at me for a minute, she would look at me anyway.

"What's a ratch?" I said, to change the subject.

"She means a rash," said Josh, who saw her come in. "Debra is allergic to flour, aren't you Debra?"

"Yes. Not all kinds though. Not the kinds you smell. Hee hee. That's a joke. Here. You want one?"

She dug into her bag and pulled out another rice cake and dropped it in front of me.

"No thank you," I said.

"They're good. This one is cheddar cheese flavored. That's my favorite. I've liked them since I was little. Do you know how old I am?" She had a steady, even voice, like the voice you hear at department stores all the time, but already I could tell that she liked to use it.

"I'll have one," said Billy, from across the room.

"Not you. Him," said Debra, pointing to me. She just about poked me in the eye with her finger, she was sitting so close.

"No, I don't," I said.

"She's the same age as me," said Susan. She was smiling again and she seemed excited to be telling somebody her age, but I still thought she looked sick, like maybe she had the flu or something. "Our birthdays are two days apart." She held up two fingers. Her hands were skinny. Almost all knuckles and bones.

"Twenty-five," I said. I was really not into guessing people's ages, especially not tonight.

"Wrong," said Debra.

"You're close," said Susan. "Go up two more." She held up her two fingers again.

"Twenty-seven," I said, feeling grateful to Susan for giving me the hint.

"Wrong," said Debra.

"Sorry. Three more," said Susan. She held up three fingers.

"Twenty-eight," I said.

"Right," said Debra. "Here, have a rice cake." My prize. She pushed the rice cake towards me again.

"Hey, you're younger than me," said Billy. "I'm twenty-nine."

"I'm twenty-seven," said Patty.

"No, thank you," I said to Debra.

"You're twenty-nine?" said Susan to Billy.

"I think I am," said Billy.

"You like them more with peanut butter?" asked Debra.

"I didn't know you were twenty-nine," said Susan to Billy.

"I've never had them with peanut butter," I said. A rice cake with peanut butter?

"I'll eat it," said Billy, who had apparently thawed his frozen hand, for he wasn't waving or shaking or doing anything with it anymore, except holding his pen. "We'll call it my birthday cake."

"Is it your birthday today?" said Susan. She was suddenly very excited, like a little kid invited to a birthday party.

"No. I just want some cake," said Billy.

"What did you have for supper?" asked Debra.

"I didn't have supper. I was watching TV."

"Can't you do both?" said Debra.

"No. My food gets too cold. I don't like eating unless it's a commercial or I'll miss the show."

"Oh," said Debra. She handed him the rice cake, and Billy started to eat it. I have no idea if she understood what he said. I know I didn't.

Everyone started to do their own thing after that. Lou returned with his coffee and settled into his chair. His back seemed to be feeling better. At least, he wasn't rubbing it anymore. Susan opened her notebook and put two pens neatly at the top of her desk. Patty slurped the rest of the juice out of her juice box and then tossed it from where she was sitting directly into the garbage can on the other side of the room.

"Nice shot," I said.

"Two points," she said. No one else seemed to notice. Beside me, Debra pulled a file out of her purse and began touching up her nails.

I tried to take stock of where I was and how I was feeling, but I was interrupted. It was no big deal. I wasn't getting anywhere anyway.

"Here, the teacher said you wanted some pop."

It was Del. She put a coffee cup in front of me.

"Just hold the cup and I'll give you some."

I took the cup. She filled it with Coke and told me to take a drink. I did. Then she poured more pop into the cup.

"That's what we used to do at the cafeteria at school," she said. "You know those drink machines where you fill your own cup? We'd stand there and fill it and drink it and fill it and drink it. Then we'd get to the cashier and let out the loudest bunch of belches you ever heard. They never charged us extra, though. I don't know why."

"Thanks," I said, hoping I wouldn't belch.

"Why don't you come up here and sit with me. This seat's usually taken, isn't it, Debra? Who usually sits here?"

The tables in the room were all two-seaters. Debra

and I were the only two sitting beside each other.

"Ross," said Debra.

"Ross. That's right. Which one's Ross?" said Del.

Debra looked around the class and then back at Del. "He's not here tonight," she said.

"Oh," said Del. "I knew that." She looked at me and winked. "Well, is he coming tonight?"

"Probably. He's always late," said Debra. "I thought I was going to be late tonight, but I wasn't."

"Why don't you come up here and sit with me?" Del said again, looking at me.

I didn't want to be thrown out of my chair again, and besides, Del seemed like the one person I could relate to so far, so I said sure and grabbed my books and went and sat with her at the front of the class.

She filled me in on everyone. Patty had Down's Syndrome. Debra, Susan, and Billy, were, to varying degrees, "intellectually challenged."

"That is the term they use today," said Del. "So I've been told, anyway. So I'm going to use it. You don't want to insult anyone."

"That's for sure," I said, for lack of anything better.

Lou, she added, calling him, "The shaggy one over there with the gray hair," dropped out of school in grade four and never went back.

"Grade four?" I said. I could not believe that anyone would drop out of school in grade four.

"It was different in those days. All the grades were in the same room. The teacher talked to everyone the same. If she didn't like you, she could make it awfully

44

uncomfortable for you. Lou there didn't get along with too many people."

I looked at him again. He was sitting in his chair, flipping through a magazine. It seemed like he was just glancing at the pictures. He was getting less and less intimidating everytime I saw him.

"How about you?" I said.

"I didn't go to high school," said Del. "I had too many more important things to do, like dating. Work.

"This is the second year that we've all been together. We talk a little about what we're doing here and what we'd like to learn. Billy wants to be a movie star. He's a real movie buff. Patty wants to write songs. She loves to sing, that one. Anne Murray. Michelle Wright."

"Can she?"

"Not at all. Couldn't carry a tune if you strapped it to her back. But she tries. It's adorable when you see it."

"What about the others? What are they here for?"

"Debra and Susan just want to write better. I'm not sure what Lou wants. He's a bit of a loner. He has a bad back so he's not always here, you know."

"And you?"

"I promised my kids I would get my high school diploma. How else am I supposed to keep them in school? So here I am. I'm fifty-three years old, I have five kids, a job, a wonderful husband, and I'm learning how to write so I can get my grade twelve. Kind of a funny way of doing things, isn't it?"

"I guess so," I said. I really didn't know what else to say. No one had ever been so upfront and honest with

45

me before. In my family, no one says anything.

"It's some group, let me tell you," she added.

"I can see that," I said. I didn't know what to think of it. At the moment, I think I could have tied all of my mom's thread together into the world's biggest knot and dropped it on her for getting me into this, but then I would have to go back to court, and who knows what kind of an essay I'd have to write for doing something like that.

Besides, nobody here was awful or anything, and I had all the Coke I could drink.

Just then Josh walked to the front of the room and said hi to everybody. Then we went around and introduced ourselves. Everybody said who they were and what they had been up to. As I gathered from Del, they all seemed to know each other, so I guessed that the whole exercise was more for my benefit than anyone else's.

When it got to my turn, I told them my name and that I was here to do some writing for an assignment I'd been given. I figured that was enough. Maybe I would tell them more later, but for now, they didn't have to know absolutely everything about me. I'm not my mother.

"What kind of assignment?" said Del.

"Just an assignment," I said. "Nothing special." I was hoping like crazy Josh wouldn't say anything.

"You mean like homework?" said Susan.

"Sort of," I said.

"Sort of like homework, eh?" said Del. You could tell she was trying to figure this out. I guess they didn't get much for excitement around here.

"Well if it's only sort of like homework, it's not from school. Now who else gives out homework that's not really homework? Oh, I know. The church. You have to do something for the church. What'dya do, steal some wine? Is the bishop making you write something about theft and all that? Good for him, if he is. I think more young people should have to do that."

"It's not the church," I said. I was starting to think that maybe I should leave. But of course, I had nowhere to go until nine o'clock.

"Oh, it's not the church," said Del.

"You stole some wine?" said Debra, who had finished with the rice cakes.

"No, I didn't steal any wine," I said.

"You musta stole something," said Lou. I was surprised to hear him get into this. He had looked very bored when I was telling everyone who I was. "You said you didn't steal any wine, but you didn't say you didn't steal anything, so you must have stole something."

"I think you're right," said Del.

"I didn't steal anything," I said. I couldn't believe I was getting into this. "I started a fire."

"Ohh, a fire," said Del. Her eyes lit up and got real big.

"Did you burn your house down?" asked Debra.

"It wasn't in the house," I said.

"Was it in the church?" she asked.

"It was at school," I said. "I started a fire at my school."

"Good for you," said Lou. "Did you burn it right down?"

"Not quite," I said. I thought he was joking, but when I turned to look at him, he wasn't.

"I burned a school down to the ground when I was a kid," said Lou. "'Course it was easier in them days. It was just a one-room schoolhouse."

"Shame on you," said Del. "Burning down a schoolhouse. There was no one inside, I hope."

"Nope," said Lou. "They got out in time."

"You're joking," said Del.

"About that last part I am," said Lou.

"Why'd you burn your school down?" asked Debra. She was talking to me again.

"Because I didn't think anyone would care what I did," I said. Then I wished I hadn't said it. It was such a sucky thing to say and especially on the first day of class.

Lucky for me no one said anything. I doubt if they even knew what I meant. Then I looked over at Lou again, and he was staring at me, and he said, "You too, eh?"

six

I could ask you to guess what our first writing assignment was and it would take you about a month before you started getting even close. It was, "My Sunday." Josh wanted us to describe what our Sundays are like. I thought to myself, what a dumb idea. Who cares what I do on a Sunday? Then I looked around, and everybody else was going crazy. Del had filled half a page before I even got my pencil case out.

"What are you writing about?" I asked her. I mean, how much could these people do on a Sunday?

"Didn't you hear? We're supposed to tell him about our Sundays. Here, lookit mine. I'm starting with getting ready to go to church. We have one bathroom in our house and five children, and four of them are girls. My oldest washes her hair in the kitchen sink. I told her, 'Good for you. That's using your head.' My little one thinks that's sick, but she never washes her hair. I practically have to tie her down to get her to do it. She doesn't like water getting in her eyes. But she's a good swimmer. So I don't know. She'll come around."

I was already beginning to learn that unless you had a lot of time, you didn't ask Del too many questions.

I started to write but stopped and erased everything. Then I started again but it sounded stupid, so I tore out the page and crumpled it up and slipped it into my pocket. I didn't want anybody picking it out of the garbage after class and reading it.

"What's the matter?" said Del. "Don't you have Sundays at your house?"

"Not really," I said. That was the truth, too. Mom always goes to work on Sundays, so it's just Dad and me at home. And he always sleeps till about ten and then goes downstairs to the TV room to watch football. We don't even eat together, unless there are leftovers in the fridge we both wanted.

Both of us are big leftover fans. Pizza, spaghetti, barbecue steak. I love having that in the morning. I like having it more in the morning than I do at night, if you want to know the truth. Mom always makes everything too fancy when we have things like steak at night. She puts all of these candles on the table and about three different forks for everybody. She even makes me drink wine, and everytime I do the very same thing. I go to the fridge and pour myself an enormous glass of milk, because that wine does absolutely nothing for my thirst.

Anyway, on a Sunday morning after a steak dinner the night before, Dad and I get to the fridge at about the same time and divvy up the leftovers. We both like the baked potatoes, too, but he's also into all of those fancy stir-fried vegetables and all of that, which I hate, so he can have s much of those as he wants. Then we go into the TV room together and sit on the couch and eat like animals.

It's so funny. Here's my dad, who every Saturday night that we eat at home together is on my case about manners and etiquette and everything else that makes eating so boring, and here he is, on the couch, in his jockey shorts and sometimes his robe, ripping meat off the T-bone with his teeth like a coyote. He gets sauce all over his face.

One time I remember, the mayor came to the door to drop something off and Dad sat and talked with him for about an hour. Then, when the mayor left, Dad went into the bathroom and saw that he had this huge glob of steak sauce on his cheek.

The rest of our Sunday is pretty ordinary. Sometimes he cuts the grass and I wash the deck or trim the hedges. Sometimes I do homework. We've gone to a movie a couple of times. When Mom gets home, we eat supper, and then her and Dad go into the living room and I go downstairs to watch TV or upstairs to read a book or something.

Mom always says the same thing to me every night. She says, "Don't you have anything you should be doing tonight?" which I always assume means, Scram, kid, so we don't spend much time together. Not that I'd want to anyway.

I decided to write about the Sundays when my brother and sister come over with their kids, but I just got going when Josh said it was time to stop writing, so everybody stopped.

Then he said, "So who wants to read theirs first?"

My eyes just about popped out of my head when heard him say that. I'm not going to read mine out loud I never show anybody anything that I write. That's wh Mom thinks I never finish anything, because I don' show it to her.

Lou said he would go first.

"On Sunday mornings I wake up and brush my teeth and go into the kitchen to eat breakfast with my wife Then we watch TV or go out for a walk. If my son come over, he comes over and we work on his car or sit aroun the kitchen table, and he tells us about how he and hi girlfriend have broken up or gotten back together. The we eat supper and go to bed."

"Thank you, Lou," said Josh. "Who's next?"

Debra's hand shot up like a bullet.

"Okay, Debra," said Josh.

"Are you ready? My Sunday by Debra Dirkson. M Sundays go like this. I wake up and take off my pajama and put on my clothes. Then I go to church with m mom and dad. We always stop for a treat on the wa home. My favorite is ice cream. Then we eat lunch an sit outside when it is nice out and visit with ou neighbors. Then my sister comes over with her kids an we play in the backyard. Then we eat supper. My mor cooks roast beef and potatoes and gravy and Yorkshir pudding. Then I watch 'Little House on the Prairie' an go to bed."

"'Little House on the Prairie,'" said Josh. "I don' think I've ever watched that show."

"It's very good. It makes me cry. Did you know Michael Landon is dead now?"

"Yes, I did know that," said Josh.

"They just have re-runs now," said Debra.

Billy wrote about falling asleep in a theater and waking up and forgetting where he was, and asking the usher for a ride home.

"What did he say?" said Lou.

"He called the police. He thought I was trying to rob him. But that was okay. They gave me a ride home."

"Were the lights flashing?" said Lou.

"I don't know," said Billy.

"I've never been in the back of a police car," said Del. "An ambulance, yes, but never a police car."

"They're nothing special," said Lou. "Just like the back of any car, except there's a cage there. I've been in the back of lots of 'em."

Susan wrote about going to the park with her friends and feeding the birds. I couldn't figure out why a person as skinny as her would want to give food away, but as my mom would say, it was none of my business.

Patty told us about driving to the lake with her mom and dad and sister, and how they all used to sing along to the music on the radio.

"Patty wants to be a singer," said Josh to me. "You love to sing, don't you, Patty?"

"Yes. I do," she said. She was smiling again.

When they were all finished, and it took awhile, believe me, Josh asked if I would like to read mine. I told him it wasn't very good or anything, but he said, "Come on. Give it a try. We'll go easy on you, won't we, guys?" and everybody in the class started saying, "Come on, Harper. We wanna hear it," and all of that.

Then Del gave me a little poke on the arm and said, "You'll do fine, don't worry. It's good. I like it."

"How do you know?" I said, covering what I had written with my arm.

"I read it while you were listening to everybody else's."

"There you go," said Josh. "Del's just going to tell us all about it anyway, so you may as well read it."

I said okay and took a deep breath. I had never even spoken in public before, much less read anything that I had written. My hands started shaking.

Dad and I spend most of our Sundays by ourselves because my mom has to go into work. Actually, she doesn't have to go in because she owns the store, but she does anyway.

The only times she doesn't work are when my brother and sister come over for a visit with their families.

My brother has two kids, Tony, aged seven, and Melissa, aged five. I call Tony Tony the Tiger because he is always sneaking up on me and jumping on my back and trying to scratch me. I call Melissa Little Miss. She always comes over in the clothes she wore to church. She is very cute, especially when she gets a stain on her white stockings. I have never seen a little kid spend more time trying to rub a stain out. Even er mother tells her not to worry about it.

My sister has one son, Martin. I call him Smartie-
Jart, because he gets 95% on everything, and be-
cause he likes Smarties. He can eat a whole box by
himself, but he always saves the last one for his dad.
My sister thinks that's because he likes to share, but I
think it's because he wants to make sure he gets
another box. He is eight years old.

One time when everyone was over for a visit, we
all went to the park and played a game of soccer.
Mom didn't want to play, so we put her in goal and
told her all she had to do was stop the ball from
getting past her. Well, do you think anyone scored a
goal that day? She was unbelievable. At one point,
after she'd gotten into the game, she ran right out of
the net and tackled my dad before he had a chance to
shoot! Little Miss thought my mom had lost her mind.
So did I, if you want to know the truth, but I think that
all the time.

We don't play soccer all the time with my brother
and sister and their families, but that was a visit that
came to my mind.

We always eat great food.

That was as far as I got. I wanted to tell them about
the way Dad eats his steak on Sunday mornings, but
like I said, I ran out of time.

"That was terrific," said Josh. "I really liked that.
You told us about your family. You were descriptive.
You stayed with the topic. Way to go, Harper."

"I liked it, too," said Del. "There was a lot of energ in it. Is that a right thing to say? I thought there was a l of energy in it."

"You can say that," said Josh.

"I liked the Smarties," said Debra.

"I like Smarties," said Susan. "I eat them all the tim before I go to bed. I have a little bowl. I have a bowl c Smarties and I eat them before I go to bed. One at time. I read, too. But it's hard to read and eat the Smart ies because I'm always looking into the bowl."

"I don't like Smarties," said Billy. "I like popcorr Great big bags of it."

"Now you're talking," said Del.

"You guys are both wrong," said Lou. "I like potat chips. I can eat a box in half an hour. My wife has t take hers to the other side of the apartment or I'll e; hers, too." Take one look at Lou, and you have to be lieve him.

Everyone went on and on about all the food the like to eat. I didn't know what to think about all c that, but then at the end of class, Josh came up and saic "See, you sure got them interested. Everybody coul see that little nephew of yours eating his Smartie and they all started thinking about the treats the like. That's good writing."

I didn't know whether I should believe him or no but when Mom came and asked if I wanted to come bac next week, I said sure. Why not? I'd spent two hours i a classroom and I didn't look at the clock even once.

seven

I sat beside Del again the next week. She told me what her four daughters and one son had been up to since last Tuesday. Then she poured me another glass of Coke, and started in again about how she and her friends used to fill and drink and re-fill and drink their pop in the lineup at the school cafeteria. She got to the part about taking their pop to the cashier before I managed to get her attention.

"I've heard this already," I said. "You told me last week."

"Oh, I'm sorry," she said. "You know I just love to talk. Sometimes I get a little carried away."

I've noticed, I said to myself. But I was still glad to be beside her, and when I sat down, she patted me on the arm with one of her pillowy soft hands and asked me how I was doing, and I felt like I could tell her anything and she wouldn't get mad or send me to my room.

Billy brought some of his popcorn. Before he let us have some, he showed us his new mitts. They were black and very big, but, as he pointed out, they kept his hands warm. Then, from his pocket, he pulled his other mitt, the one that he had worn the week before, and told us, "Next time I'm on a bus with my friends, here's our football." He had a smile that stretched from one piece of tape on the side of his glasses to the other.

Then he invited us to take a napkin and put some popcorn on it.

Josh walked in and helped himself. I have never seen a teacher mix with the students the way he does. He talks with everyone all the time and never gets mad. I know I've only been here for a week, but Del said that she's never seen him ticked off or upset either. He dresses like the rest of us. Tonight he was wearing the same jeans and runners he wore last week with a new sweater. He smiled when he saw me and asked how I was doing.

When everyone was sitting at their desks, Josh went to the front of the class and told us we would be writing stories tonight. Soap Operas, to be precise.

"Now who knows something about soap operas?" he said.

"I do," said Susan. She was as bright-eyed and pale as the week before. I know that's a funny combination, but that is how she looks. "I watch them all day, before I go to work." She was eating her popcorn like a bird — one piece at a time, her skinny fingers darting from her napkin to her mouth like a sparrow pecking seed from a feeder.

"What can you tell us about them?"

"They're very pretty. Everybody is very pretty." She nodded when she talked. Her whole body practically bobbed up and down with her head.

"Even the men?"

"The men are pretty, too," she said.

Josh wrote the word "Pretty" on the board at the front of the room.

"Who else knows something about soap operas?"

"I like Cricket," said Debra. She did not have any rice cakes with her tonight. When she saw me she said, "You start any fires since the last time I saw you?" She didn't seem to be joking or anything. She asked as if she really wanted to know. Then again, she seems to ask about a lot of things that she really wants to know.

"No, I managed to get through the whole week," I said.

"Good for you," she said. "You like my jacket? It's new. My mom bought it for me."

She was wearing the same wild jacket as the week before. I told her, "Yes, I do like it."

"Does your mom buy you jackets sometimes?"

"Sometimes," I said. Like everyday, I could have added, but I didn't. I never wear the things she brings home.

"What's a Cricket?" said Billy.

"Is that a person?" said Josh.

"She's my favorite. She's on 'The Young and the Restless.' She has long blonde hair and is very beautiful. Except Paul didn't want to marry her after Danny moved to New York. He stood her up in the hospital. It was very sad. My mom said I shouldn't watch it anymore, but I do anyways. I get very upset sometimes."

"Okay, Debra has hit on something else here that's very important," said Josh. He wrote "Plot twists" on the board. "What does plot have to do with a story?" he said.

"It's what the story is about," said Debra. "We took that last time."

"And what is 'The Young and the Restless' about?" he said.

"It's about anything," said Lou, who was looking as ragged as ever. I had never seen such long gray hair on a man before. Not that it was down to his shoulders or anything, but most people, at least the ones I know, when their hair turns gray, they either cut it short or it starts falling out. But old Lou, his hair was long as ever, and that old green ball cap was still stuck on his head, as if it never came off.

Maybe that's why he never gets his hair cut. He can't get his cap off his head.

"People getting married, divorced," he went on. "People making money. Everybody knows everybody. Nobody likes each other."

He really seemed to know quite a bit about these soap operas.

"That's right," said Josh, and he wrote "Anything" on the board, then beneath that he wrote the words "married", "divorced," and "money."

"Anything else, Lou?" he said.

"No. I don't like watching them much myself. The wife does all the time. Only parts I like are when they're hanging around the swimming pool."

I was taking notes but I stopped and put my pen down. It's not like we were going to be tested on this stuff, so I don't even know why I was taking notes in the first place. Habit, I guess. I always take about a million pages of notes at school. Of course, I never look at them again, but I sure have them.

Mom watches the soaps all the time. When Dad's out she watches "The Young and the Restless" after supper. I tape it for her on the VCR every afternoon. I show her how to do it practically everyday, but she always throws her hands in the air and says, "I don't know how to work those things. I'd just mess it up. You do it for me."

You can tell she just doesn't want to do it. In the first place, I was with her when she bought the thing, so I was right there when she started telling the salesman what he should know about the products he sells. And I saw how she talked the guy down about a hundred and fifty bucks on the price.

In the second place, she has a sewing machine the size of a small airplane in her sewing room in the basement, and when she gets the thing all lit up and spinning and churning, it looks like it's going to eat the entire house. That or wrap the place in thread.

Sometimes she pulls out the ironing board and irons while she watches. Other times she just sits on the couch with a cup of tea and takes it all in. I've never figured out how a woman like my mom could spend two minutes watching a cheesy soap opera, but she does practically every night.

I sit with her sometimes, if I'm bored, which is always,

but usually I stay upstairs and read. When I do sit with her, I drive her nuts asking who that guy is and who he's married to now, and who that woman is. I know all about Cricket being stood up by Paul at the hospital. He's a jerk. Mr. Big Private Detective. So is Danny, her ex-husband, if you want to know the truth. He was this singer and every once in a while they would show one of his concerts. They were awful. They weren't ever rock n' roll.

My favorite guy is Victor Newman. He's this rich guy whose been married to just about everybody in the show, and everytime somebody tries to muscle in on him, like Jack, who couldn't comb his lovely hair without his dad helping him out, Victor comes out on top.

The only thing I don't like about him is he always talks in this whisper, and his head is always tilted down. So to look someone in the eye, he has to raise his eyebrows and crinkle his forehead. It's kind of hard to describe, actually, and it looks so stupid. I don't know why he always does that.

Mom likes Jill Abbott because "she is her own person." Yeah right, is what I say. If my sister ever carried on like Jill Abbott, Mom would have her locked in her room upstairs until she was ninety-five.

"She has such spunk," Mom says. "Look at her. She doesn't take guff from any man. She stands right up to them. Good for her."

She stands up to them when she's not lying down with them, is what I say, but not to Mom. She'd kill me if I said anything like that to her.

62

"So let's get going on it then," said Josh. "I want you to write your own soap opera. You can invent your very own or pick up on one of the shows on TV."

"Oh goody," said Debra. "I'm going to get Paul and Cricket back together again."

"Can we use people from the movies?" said Billy. His popcorn was all gone now. It was the saltiest popcorn I'd ever had in my life. Mom would have had him arrested for attempted murder if she had tasted it. "He tried to clog my son's arteries with salt," I could hear her say to the detective. "The proof is right there in the bowl. Look at it. Look at it!"

Everyone else thought it was great.

"Sure you can," said Josh.

I got started on mine right away. I like this kind of stuff, writing stories and that. At school, all we ever write are essays and lab reports. Even in English class. We read all of these great books, then the teacher tells us to write an essay about them. Why not write a story? I mean, it's great to know what things like plot mean, but isn't the whole point of school to teach you how to actually *do* something? I mean, what's the point of knowing what a plot is if you're never going to write a story?

That's one of the many problems I have with school, but no one I talk to ever listens. Even Ms. Davis, the counsellor, says I should just do the work and stop questioning everything. The thing is, I don't actually question *anything*. I just get ticked off that we have to do it, then I get bored, so I don't do it, and I fail.

Dad thinks I'm stupid. He wants to send me to every

tutor in the country. He's always coming home saying things like, "You know, I was talking with Lloyd Connors today, and his daughter Connie is studying mathematics at the university. I wonder if she'd be willing to give Harper a hand?"

Can you believe it? Connie Connors. What a lousy name. It's like John Johnson or Tom Thomson. I would hate to have a name like that. Even with the name I have I would hate to have a name like that.

But anyway, my parents never actually ask me if I want a tutor, and they have certainly never taken the time to talk to me about my attitude towards school. They just set me up with some person who walks into my life and tries to help me understand math better, or science, or whatever, assuming that I need the help.

"We are hiring you to turn grape juice into wine," I heard Dad say to one tutor he hired. He was quite proud of himself for that one. I'm sure he has it written down somewhere.

I have already mentioned what I think about wine, so to say the least, Dad's prize catch failed miserably.

My brother and sister breezed through school. I don't even think they would know what a B or a C looks like if they hadn't had alphabet wallpaper in their rooms. (Isn't that cute? A helpful and fun way to learn your letters, Mom used to say. I put posters of the Starship Enterprise up when I moved into my brother's room. Of course, Dad tore them down.)

My brother still says, "Only an idiot could fail high school," knowing full well that at this very moment, I am about one percentile away from flunking out of all of my courses. "At least I don't cheat," I said the last time he was over. My brother was nearly expelled from university for cheating on an exam. He had to rewrite it by himself and if he didn't achieve a certain mark, he was gonzo. That was quite the little scandal around our house.

"Alright, that's enough," Dad said, looking like he was going to huff and puff and blow my head through the roof.

It was a mean thing to say, I know, but I didn't exactly start it.

Anyway, a soap opera was just the thing for me to write, and with all the flakes and phonies I know at school, I had no problem coming up with the characters.

I mean, I don't exactly walk home from school everyday wishing I could be more popular, or, that I could pal around with guys from the rugby team, who make cavemen seem like Law Professors when they're out in public, or, that I had a girlfriend. Not if you're talking about the people I go to school with.

They make the cast of "Beverly Hills, 90210" look like Archie and Veronica.

We all finished our stories at practically the same time. Josh went to the front of the class and asked who would like to read first and everyone put their hand up. I guess that tells you how excited everyone was about this assignment.

Del offered Josh free pop, so he chose her.

"Okay, here it is," she said, and she began to read.

"Paul wanted to marry Cricket, but when he got to

the hospital to visit his ailing father, he fell in love with his father's doctor, a woman named Sarah, so he stood Cricket up at the altar.

"Cricket was devastated, but not for long, for in the crowd at her wedding was her cousin Antonio, who had connections with the mob. 'Get him,' she told Antonio. But Antonio did not want to leave the wedding. He had fallen in love with Mary-Lou, one of Cricket's bridesmaids. So Cricket told Mary-Lou that Antonio wanted to take her for a drive, and so Mary-Lou and Antonio went for a drive to look for Paul.

"In the meantime, Paul's father discovers that his doctor and new daughter-in-law, Sarah, was giving him the wrong medication.

"Their story goes way back. When Paul's father was a young man coming home from the war, he fell in love with a woman named Kate. She was a nurse. Since he was already married at the time to Paul's mother, and did not want to divorce her, he had an affair. Kate became pregnant, and he took off. But the second he saw Sarah, he was reminded of Kate, and after a few days in the hospital, he figured it out. Sarah was his daughter!

"Antonio and Mary-Lou find Paul and Sarah in the cafeteria at the hospital. They are eating a sandwich. Paul sees Antonio and dives for cover. Sarah, who knows Paul is her stepbrother and wants him out of the picture, turns to see a gun pointed at her head, but as soon as Antonio sees Sarah, he puts his gun down.

"Sarah had treated Antonio when he was in the hospital two years before with gout. He had promised her then that if she made him feel better, he would never do anything to her.

"While those two are talking, Paul slips out the back door and gets into his car and drives to a new town. What he doesn't know is that Cricket is in the backseat.

"To Be Continued."

"Wow," said Josh when Del finished.

"You confused me, so it must be pretty good," said Lou.

"How did Cricket get in the backseat of Paul's car with her wedding dress on?" asked Debra. Here come the questions. You could almost see her eyes lighting up.

"She must have had extra clothes," said Susan, who was just as excited. She was waving her hand in the air to get Josh's attention. "Is that right? She had extra clothes? I've been to a wedding where the bride had extra clothes. She got changed at the hotel, and then they went on their honeymoon. They went to Hawaii. I've never been there. I've been to Disneyland, but never to Hawaii. Maybe next year."

One thing I was starting to notice about Susan was, she talks like she eats — in little pecks.

"I've been to Hawaii," said Debra. "It's too hot. I got a sunburn and had to stay in the hotel."

"She didn't have extra clothes. She got in Paul's car with her wedding dress on. What's so hard to believe about that?" said Del.

"How did she get to the hospital?" asked Debra.

"She took a cab."

"How did she pay for the cab?"

"She took her purse."

"What color was her purse? Was it white?"

"Oh brother. Yes, it was white. She had a white purse."

"Was it a big purse or a little purse?"

"It was a huge purse with a ton of money in it. She gave the cabbie a huge tip," said Del. I think she was getting tired of the questions.

"What's a tip?" said Susan. "I've heard of that before. At work they're always saying, 'Did you get a tip?' and I never know what they're talking about."

"A tip is extra money you give a person for doing a good job," said Lou. "Like you give a waitress a tip if the toast isn't warmer than the coffee and the eggs she gives you aren't running all over your plate."

I could see Lou sitting in places where you could drink your coffee through a straw it's so cold, and you have to catch the eggs before you can eat them. One of those All Night Diner places. I've never been to one myself. My parents prefer having brunch at Marcel's or Eggs Benedict at the CP Hotel. Fancy places where Dad meets all of his important friends and brings them over to the table to say hello.

I should take Mom and Dad to one of the places Lou eats at and bring him over to say hello to them. It would probably bring on the first case of simultaneous heart attacks ever recorded in Edmonton.

"I've never had a tip before then," said Susan. She works in a restaurant somewhere. She works in the kitchen.

"A tip can also be a piece of advice or information,"

aid Josh. "Like in Del's story, if someone had given
Paul a tip that Antonio was coming to the hospital to get
him, Paul would have left sooner."

"How would he have left sooner?... in a car?" asked
Debra.

"That was just an example," said Josh. "You can ask
Del later. Who wants to read next?"

I said I would. I was dying to read mine, if you want
to know the truth, so I started reading before anyone
could start talking again. In this class, you never know
when they're going to finish, if they ever do finish.

"Okay, my soap is called 'One Life Too Many' and
his episode is 'The Garden Party.'"

*It was to be the event of the year. Toby Garden's
Christmas Party. Everyone who is anyone at Emville
Senior High would be there. Prom Queen Joanna
Martin. Quarterback Newt Wisen. Cheerleaders
Sheri-Lyn Johnson and Martha Cooper. All-Province
basketball star Tiny McGill.*

*The party was to take place at the very expensive
and marvelous home of Mr. and Mrs. James Garden,
he of the Garden, Winter & Snow Law Firm, and she
of the very prestigious Rose Garden Restaurant, where
two can dine for twenty bucks plus a fat tip.*

*The high school cafeteria was abuzz with excite-
ment weeks before the big night. Hair salons were busier
than on New Year's Eve. Local clothiers reported
record sales. Only the teachers had a complaint — the
students were dutifully attending class, but no one's*

mind was on their work.

As the date of the party approached, Rose Garden and her meticulously trained staff at the Rose Garden Restaurant spent hours of overtime receiving and sorting the "Will Be Attending" cards that accompanied each of the 225 invitations.

The caterers had been chosen well in advance, as had the band and various solo entertainers. Security had been arranged, donated actually, by one of James Garden's clients, the owner of a small commercial-property security outfit, who had been charged, but found not guilty due to insufficient evidence, of theft over $10,000.

All was set and ready to go when two days before the party a serious problem presented itself to the organizing committee.

Toby Garden had forgotten to send himself an invitation. Estelle Rabner, one of Rose Garden's excellent assistants, discovered the faux pas *while cross-referencing the seating arrangements with the color schemes of the various party rooms.*

Rose Garden could not believe what she heard, so she quickly double-checked Ms. Rabner's work, and then promptly fired the woman for butting into affairs that were none of her business. Rose then called her husband, and told him the news. Mr. Garden hurried home immediatly after his golf game and a few martinis with the boys in the clubhouse.

James Garden, ever the cool head during times of intense crisis, called his partners and conferred over

*the phone. The news was bad: No invite; no party. It
was written right there in the constitution.*

*Toby Garden was devastated. He took up smoking
and went to school without washing his hair. His
closest friends tried consoling him but when they
heard what he had done, they scrammed, knowing full
well that to be seen with him would do nothing to help
them get into college the following year.*

*The day of the party arrived and although the
enthusiasm and excitement for it had dimmed some-
what in light of the recent events, that did not stop the
limousines from pulling into the lanes commonly
reserved for school buses to shuttle the party-goers to
their homes, and then on to the Garden Party.*

*Toby sat in his room and watched as limo after
limo pulled up in front of his parents' house. There
was The Quarterback, big Newt Wisen, football in
hand, as usual, and a fabulous red and gold tuxedo to
match the helmet that he wore proudly on his head.
Tony Woods, class valedictorian, handing out copies of
his speech, and excerpts from his first book, entitled,
I'm On Top, Where Are You?. Vanessa Charmaine, a
fashion model who has already posed semi-clad in the
most recent Wal-Mart flyers (she was wearing pajamas).
And of course, Dorothy Burnett, the Queen of Gossip,
whose column "Do Tell" in the school newspaper has
been rated the most widely read piece of writing in the
school's long and celebrated history.*

*Toby watched with disgust but inside his little head
he had a plan. A monstrous plan that would show*

everyone who dared to turn their backs on him that he, Toby Garden, was not someone you turned your back on, unless you were going somewhere and he was staying.

Toby was going to crash his own party. It would be so easy. He had been in on all of the planning sessions and meetings. He knew where the food was stored and how, with one quick dump of a thick gooey chemical he was sure he could find somewhere, he could turn his parents' prized hot tub into a cauldron of thick, chunky soup. And he knew exactly which switch on the circuit breaker could put an end to the music.

The only thing was, with so many people milling around, Toby did not know how he could slip outside. He knew how to get in — he had a key to all of the doors — but he was not sure how to get out, and until he got out, he could not get back in to do his dastardly deeds.

Well, to cut to the quick, Toby need not have worried. The party of the year was not a party at all. Rose Garden forgot to order pointy hats and noise-makers, putting most of the revellers out of their comfort zone right off the bat.

Sir Duke Security failed to show, leaving James Garden as the lone chaperone, which was too much responsibility for one person, especially since he had to take his briefcase, cordless phone, daytimer, port-able fax machine, copies of The Financial Post, The New York Daily News, *and the* Emville Eyeopener, *and his secretary, Ms. Bambi LaRouche, with him wherever he went.*

And finally, Joanna Martin and Vanessa Charmaine wore the same outfits, and that was a killer. Joanna still gets upset to this day whenever someone mentions the party, and Vanessa has refused to speak to her mother except to ask for more allowance.

"This concludes my story."

I stopped reading and looked around the room. Everyone was nodding and sort of smiling, as if to offer their approval, but no one said anything, until Debra said, "I've never been invited to a party either."

"I have," said Susan. "I have a friend who invited me to her birthday party. It was fun. I had a good time."

"Not me," said Debra.

"This isn't a story about not getting invited to a party," I said.

"Maybe not, but that's what it sounds like," said Del.

eight

I took it with me when I went to see Ms. Davis. She was so excited when I told her I had written an entire story and read it in front of the class. She even gave me a hug. Then she asked me what was wrong. I guess she could tell that she was the only excited person in the room. So I handed her my story and asked her to read it. She did. I asked her what she thought and she said pretty much the same thing that Del and Debra and everyone else said last night.

What a bummer that was.

"I'm not even in the story," I said. "How can it be about me when I'm not even in it?"

"Well, you did write it," she said. "Perhaps there is bitterness inside you towards some of your classmates that came out on its own in your story.

"I mean. It's very good," she went on, after I didn't say anything for about two minutes. "It's very funny and imaginative. It's also very accurate. I know some of the people you talk about and you hit the nail right on the head with all of them."

She was trying to make me feel good. I hate it when people do that. I mean, if they really wanted to make you feel good, they wouldn't have made you feel so bad in the first place. So I let her have it right back.

"But it's full of bitterness and spite because even though there is no character in there with my name or even a slight resemblance to me, it's about me, right? Somehow it's about me."

I was feeling really ticked off. Last night after class Josh had said the exact same thing to me. He said that whenever you write something down, a little bit of yourself goes with it, no matter whether you want it to or not. So I said, Okay, fine, where is Del in that little thing she wrote? Which character is she — Sarah the killer doctor? Cricket? Paul the Louse?

"That's a little bit different," he said. "She was following someone else's script. You invented your own."

"Oh, of course," I said. "That's different."

"I am just suggesting that you may have some resentment inside that has to come out," said Ms. Davis, who I am suddenly getting very tired of very quickly. "Maybe writing is a way of exploring that."

So now I'm an explorer all of a sudden. What does she want me to do — seek new frontiers? Boldly go where no kid my age has ever gone before? It's a stupid story I wrote in a stupid writing class. Now everyone sees it as my autobiography.

I went home and for the first time since I started going, Mom asked to see what I've been doing at "The Cafe." She still uses that goofy French accent of hers when she

75

says "cafe." It's really starting to make me sick.

I told her I didn't have anything to show her. The last thing I need is her expert analysis.

"You know your essay is due in two weeks," she said. "You better get started on it."

Like she cares if I get it done or not. I heard her talking on the phone the other night and all I heard her say about me was, "Oh Harper? He's fine. Oh yes. That's all behind him now. He's doing well at school again. Ben is thinking of taking him skiing this Christmas, if he can get the time off. He's been so busy lately ... " Blah, blah, blah.

I'm fine, am I Mom? I'm doing well at school again? When was the last time I did well at school? Grade four? No. I almost failed grade four because I didn't get along with the teacher. He said I was a spoiled brat because I got a ride to school instead of taking the bus. Grade two? No, it wasn't grade two. You went with Dad to some seminar or something in Europe, and decided to stay for six weeks and left me with some nanny who couldn't fluff a pillow without taking a belt of gin first.

Kindergarten? Maybe it was kindergarten. I don't seem to recall any difficulties there. I guess maybe you're right, Mom. I'm sorry. I have done well at school before — in kindergarten. I did very well. I learned my alphabet and everything. Best of all, I still remember most of it.

And Dad's taking me skiing? But only if he can get the time off, right? Okay, well, I won't hold my breath, because the last time Dad thought of taking me somewhere was when we were going to go canoeing, but something came up, didn't it? I can't remember … Oh yes, I do remember! He went with someone else. That's right. He went with Dr. Copperton instead. Dad couldn't get any time off to go during the entire two months that I was out of school in the summer, but every one of his patients cancelled all of their appointments during the first week of September, and he went with Dr. Copperton. Just my luck! Oh well, maybe next life.

Gosh, that must be hard on poor old Dad, making all these plans to get away with his son, only to have to change them all around to meet the needs of his patients. He's such a dedicated man. And when he's not handing out medication or checking old people's blood pressure, he's at meeting after meeting, and rally after rally, representing "his town" as the top vote-getter in the latest municipal election.

He really is an inspiration to us all.

I am very impressed. Almost as much as I am with the startling insight and scintillating communication skills of my new "friends" at the Cafe. Speaking of them, I wonder what they will accuse me of next? Maybe they'll call me a thief because I wrote about a kid who wanted to break into his own house, or, a delinquent because I wrote about kids under twenty-one smoking cigarettes.

If they do, I'll have to tell them that I have already been called a delinquent in my life, so they will have to come up with something better.

I didn't say a word to Mom the whole time we were driving from our house to the Cafe in the city. I didn't pretend to read or anything either. I just sat there, hoping she would get the message.

When we got there she said, while checking her short and sassy hairdo in the rearview mirror, "Same time? Nine o'clock?"

"No," I said. "We're going all night tonight. Sort of a dusk-to-dawn thing, like the movies."

She just shook her head and shifted the car into drive.

A very astute woman, my mother. Maybe if I wrapped myself in fabric and put a sale sticker on my forehead she'd notice me. Of course, she'd try to talk me down in price first, or look for a better deal somewhere else.

nine

I sat beside Del again, but I made it pretty clear that I was ticked off with her. She asked me if I wanted a Coke and I said no. Not "No thanks" or anything like that, just, "No." I didn't even look at her when I said it. I just sat there with my arms folded and stared at my desk. Then Susan came by with some chocolate chip cookies she had made and asked me if I wanted one.

"No, thanks. I'm full of resentment. Maybe next week."

That got her all flustered. She began acting like a little bird again, fluttering around my desk and chirping away about how she burned most of the cookies, and it was a new recipe, so they probably would not have turned out anyway. Then she apologized for offering them to me. Her face was as red as a wagon.

I told her it wasn't her or her cookies I was mad at, but she didn't believe me. She went and sat down and didn't offer them to anyone else.

Billy made her feel better though. He walked over and took about six of them. Then Lou leaned over and scooped a couple off the plate. He would need about twenty to fill his gut. I know that's not a nice thing to say, but that's the way I'm feeling tonight. I don't like any of these people anymore.

"Aren't we in a lovely mood today," said Del after Susan left.

"I didn't know we were a couple," I said.

"What's the matter with you? Somebody beat you up at school?"

"Oh, is that something else my story is about, being a weakling? If all you guys are so observant, what are you doing in this nuthouse learning how to write? You should be out working somewhere."

"My, my. You better pick up that bottom lip of yours before someone trips over it. We'll never hear the end of it if that happens."

"What?"

"You're pouting. Don't you know you're pouting? It's written all over your face."

"I'm not pouting."

"Sure you are. Hey Lou, come over here. Does he look like he's pouting to you?"

"Don't call Lou," I said.

"I can see from here," said Lou, cookie crumbs falling all over his shirt. "I've driven over speed bumps smaller than that bottom lip of his."

"There, see? Lou thinks you're pouting."

"Lou's wrong."

"How about Debra. Debra, come over here. Does he look like he's pouting to you?"

Debra was the absolute last person I wanted involved with this. She would turn my mood into another game of Twenty Questions. But after Del called her, she walked over and practically stuck her nose right in my face.

"What are you pouting for?" she said.

"I'm not pouting," I said. I uncrossed my arms and sat up a bit in my chair.

"Del thinks you're pouting."

"So does Lou," said Del.

"I think so too," said Debra.

"Great. Can we get a few more people over here? Maybe someone from down the hall?" I said.

"What are you pouting for?" asked Debra, again.

"Nothing."

"Are you mad because we didn't like your story?"

"I don't care what you like."

"Maybe you'd like to do it again."

"I don't think so."

"Have you ever been invited to a party before?"

"Am I under arrest here or what? What's with all the questions?"

"I just want to know if you've ever been invited to a party before."

Everybody was just sort of sitting or standing around waiting for Debra and me to finish our scintillating conversation. Even Josh was just standing at the front of the room, pretending to sort some papers. Del was looking at me like I was going to break down or something.

"No, I haven't," I said. "Are you happy now?"

"No," said Debra, rubbing her stomach all of a sudden. "I have a stomachache. I ate too much spaghett for supper."

She stuck her tongue out for dramatic effect, as i she was going to barf.

Then Josh started the class. He told us, "Tonight is an Open Night, so you can write about anything you want."

Everyone got pretty excited about that.

Patty stopped the Anne Murray tape she plays on her Walkman every class and shouted, "It's about time!" with a big grin on her face, and Billy pounded his desk three times with his fist. Then, in typical, bad-acting fashion, he rubbed his hand and winced, as if he had just put it through a brick wall.

I guess these "Open Nights" were something pretty special.

In a flash Billy and Patty had joined together with Lou and were looking at the last edition of *The Popsicle Journal* to find out what they wrote about last month. I could hear them talking. Billy wanted to write about horses. He had seen one on television last night that, in his words, "would just not leave my mind."

"You dreamt about a horse last night?" said Lou, who was helping himself to more of Susan's cookies. Maybe he was going to eat twenty of them.

"As a matter of fact, no, I didn't," said Billy. "I dreamt about canoeing down a river in a boat. But when I got to the other side, there was a horse waiting for me. So maybe I did dream about a horse last night. I guess it depends what time I actually got to the other side of the river."

"I'm gonna dream about these cookies," said Lou. He was starting to go through them pretty quickly.

Susan took that as the compliment it was and became all fluttery again, and blushed, and told Lou that she could make him some more if he really wanted, but he would have to wait two weeks because she was working every night for the next seven days.

"I'll wait," said Lou.

Then Susan went into the library to look for some recipe books.

Debra pulled a book from her purse and started to read. It was a mystery, naturally. There's always lots of questions in a mystery, and when Josh asked what she planned on writing about tonight, she told him that as soon as she was finished reading, she was going to write a mystery of her own.

Del started in on a letter she wanted to get done. I figured I may as well start my stupid essay.

I couldn't get going on it, though. I didn't know how to start, and besides, I felt like I wanted to talk first. I've felt like this before, but I never really had anyone around to say anything to. Plus I felt kind of bad about barking at Del and everyone the way I did.

"Did you ever get invited to parties?" I said to Del.

It took her about a millisecond to forget about her letter.

"Me? Oh sure, I was always invited to parties. My mom wouldn't let me go to them though. She thought I would get into trouble."

"Did you ever go anyway?"

"No, but I still got into trouble. I had my first child when I was sixteen."

"That's one year older than I am right now," I said. I thought for a second about me being someone's dad. Not a pretty picture.

"Pretty young, isn't it? She turned out okay though. I don't know how, but she did. All my kids are okay now, and I have a wonderful husband who has a job, and I go to church. That's all I need."

I thought about something for a minute, then I said, "Why did you get pregnant?"

Del looked at me.

"You mean, 'Why did I go out and do exactly what I knew my mother was afraid of me doing?'"

"Yeah."

"I wanted to get back at her. Stupid, isn't it? I get back at my mother by having a baby."

"That's why I started that fire," I said.

"I thought you said you started it because no one cared?"

"I may have said that, but I knew my parents would care. My dad is a town councillor. Of course he would care if his son set a fire in the new high school. And my mom is a businesswoman. She talks to people in town everyday. She'd care if I set a fire."

"So they would care, but not about you, is that what you're saying?"

"That's it," I said.

"And did it work? Did you get back at them?"

"Are you kidding? The only reason my dad isn't

84

rime Minister is because the newspapers didn't print
ny name. Mom probably had the best month of busi-
ess in her life. There were people coming to the house
o try on her dresses. Everybody felt so sorry for them.
t was sickening."

"Uh-huh. And you're left with an essay to write and
was left with a baby. You know what we should have
one? We should have gone to our parents and said,
Hey, I've got something I want to say to you. Sit down
nd hear me out.'"

"I don't think that would have worked," I said.

"I'll bet it would. I found that out as soon as I be-
ame a mother. The baby would want something, she'd
ry, and I'd get it for her. When she became a toddler,
he'd start pulling on my pant leg or yapping about this
r that, and I'd know she wanted something right away. But
s soon as she became a teenager, the messages stopped
oming. She wouldn't say anything to me anymore.

"I had to tell her, 'Listen, if you've got a problem,
ome to me and tell me what it is. Otherwise, knock it
ff. I'm not a fortune teller. You want me to look in a
rystal ball everytime you're in a bad mood, you better
uy me the ball first, so I can look at it.' My daughter
hought I was crazy. She said, 'You think I'm gonna
uy you a crystal ball with my allowance?'"

"Did it work?"

"She's not pregnant. She has a job. She has a boy-
riend. She finished school."

"I don't think that would work with my parents," I
aid.

"You might be surprised," said Del.

"I would have to be very surprised," I said.

I ended up writing this stupid thing called "A Letter to Mom & Dad." It was Josh's idea. He came and asked us how we were doing and Del told him about everything we were talking about. I don't know why mothers do that all the time. It's like, if they're going to say anything, they have to say everything.

Anyway, Josh suggested that I write a letter. "You have to write the essay, right? So tonight you can practice writing about your family. Write about anything you want, but make it about them."

So I wrote the letter. It went like this:

Dear Mom and Dad:

Hi. How are you? I'm fine. Well, not really, but my head's not falling off or anything, and I haven't started a fire in almost a month, so that's good.

I am writing you this letter because my teacher said I should. Actually, I'm writing this because Del, this woman I sit beside in my writing class, said she would sic Debra and Susan on me if I didn't. They are these two women in my class. Debra is the World's Greatest Question Asker and Susan likes to comment on everything everyone says. She bakes good cookies though, so I've heard.

It could be worse. She could have sent Lou over to sit on me, or asked me to go to the movies with Billy and see how long it takes us to get driven home in a police car.

Anyway, I'm writing this letter to let you know that I'm not a delinquent or stupid or lazy, and that I didn't start that fire to burn the school down. I just feel really empty.

I know that's no reason to start a fire, but it's how I feel.

Bye for now. Hope to see you soon. Say hi to the kids.

Harper

ten

The next day was another meeting day with Ms. Davis. Meaning it was another day when I had to go to her office and sit outside her door until whoever was inside meeting with her before me left. And then wait some more until she invited me in with that big, happy smile of hers that I was starting to get really tired of. So that is what I did.

After we sat down, I told her what Del had said. I didn't tell her like, "Listen to this great idea someone told me! I'm going to start telling my parents how I feel!" I just sort of told her.

She said, "I think that is a wonderful idea," and got all excited. "I think that is one of the things you can put in your essay — that you are going to start communicating more effectively with your parents."

I got out my pen and wrote that down. "Communicate more effectively with my parents." A very fancy phrase, if you ask me. "You got anymore of those?" I said.

"You try that one first," she said.

The next thing I did was I showed her my letter. I

just reached into my pocket and handed it to her. She didn't know what it was, but then she read it and you could tell she was surprised. I mean, it's not like I'd bared my soul or anything, but compared to crying over an imaginary dog, it was quite a step.

"Have you shown your mom and dad this?" she said.

"Are you kidding?"

"I think they need to see this."

"I think they'd rather see me on a bus to the North Pole."

"Harper, give your parents some credit. They don't know what to do with you. I talk to them on the phone every week. Your mother keeps saying, 'Have you come up with anything yet?' They're worried about you, Harper. They just have no idea what's going on in your head."

"They've never told me that."

"Well, you're not exactly the easiest person to talk to, you know. You've barged out of here everytime you've come in. You said yourself you spend most of your time at home in your room."

"That's because there's no one around to do anything with," I said. I was getting a little ticked off again. It's like all of a sudden, I'm the problem, and my parents have nothing to do with it.

"Have you ever asked them to do anything with you?"

"Yeah. We go down to the arcade all the time. My dad's a real pinball freak. Mom likes the record store. She goes nuts over rap, except the guys in the store always tease her because she has her clothes on backwards."

"I don't get it."

"Don't get what?"

"I don't get the 'clothes on backwards' bit. What is that supposed to mean?"

"Don't you watch MuchMusic? They have videos of these rap bands that wear their clothes backwards. It's their thing. It's like painting their faces or shaving their heads."

Ms. Davis took a deep breath and looked away from me for a minute. I don't know if she got the thing about the clothes on backwards or not, but she seemed to be reaching the end of her line, patience-wise.

But you know what? I didn't care. I mean, what does she think I'm supposed to do — make my parents my best friends? If she wants me to do that, we may as well end these little meetings of ours right now.

"What about at school?" she said. She seemed to be okay again. "Do you ever ask anyone to do things with you at school?"

"I don't have to ask anyone to do anything with me at school. They do it to me anyway. Last week Darren Talbot ripped two chapters out of my math book. I had to look through every garbage can in the school before I could study for my test. Then everybody wonders why I fail all the time."

"Are you as sarcastic and distant with your class-mates and parents as you are with me?"

I looked at her to see if she was joking, then I looked around the office to see if maybe someone else had slipped in behind me. Nope.

"What?" I said. I wasn't being sarcastic. She was asking me stupid questions so I was giving her stupid answers, just like the rule says.

"You can be very sarcastic with people, Harper, and very distant. You stay in your room at home. You eat lunch by yourself at school. You do not take part in any extracurricular activities. But look at the way things are going for you at this writing class. You're making friends. You're being creative and introspective. I was talking to your instructor there the other day and he said you were doing fine. So what is it? Why are you doing so well there and not anywhere else?"

"Maybe it's because half of them can't tie their own shoes," I said. Then I really wish I hadn't said it. I thought about Debra eating those stupid rice cakes so she wouldn't get a "ratch," and Patty sitting there in her own little desk listening to her music. She smiles at me every class now, and last week she walked up to me and said, "You can sit beside me now if you want," which is a very long way from, "You're in my seat." And she hasn't said one more thing about the clothes I wear, which I take to be a compliment.

"I don't know why," I said. I was feeling pretty lousy all of a sudden.

"Well, think about it," said Ms. Davis. You could tell she was a little upset.

eleven

When I got home after school, Mom and Dad were sitting at the kitchen table waiting for me. I walked into the kitchen and saw them and just about fainted. I hadn't seen Mom and Dad sitting at the kitchen table waiting for me to come home from school since my grandma died eight years ago.

"Did someone die?" I said. I got a little bit scared just thinking about it.

Mom shook her head and Dad rolled his eyes.

"Your mother sprained her ankle at work today," he said. "She can't walk."

I looked a little bit closer at Mom and saw that her face was all white. She looked sick, if you want to know the truth. Her feet were up on one of the chairs. Her right foot had a big bandage on it.

"How'd that happen?" I said.

"I fell off the stool your father bought me for Christmas last year. I was trying to reach a hat for Gladys Cartwright. Her son is getting married next month."

"Who's he marrying?" asked Dad.

"I don't know," said Mom. You could tell she didn't feel like talking about it.

"Did it hurt?" I said. I know it's a stupid question, but what else am I supposed to say — where's your other shoe?

"Of course, it hurt," said Mom. She seemed to know that it was a stupid question, too.

"Sprains are more painful than breaks," said Dad, Mr. Authority Figure.

I wiped that thought out of my head. I wasn't going to be like that tonight, calling my dad names and everything. I was going to be nice, so I could prove to Ms. Davis that it was them, not me, who had the problems.

It would be hard, especially with Dr. Dad wearing his this-is-very-serious face, even though, when I sprained my finger last summer and my uncle said, "You should be more careful when you sit down," Dad laughed for about an hour and never did get anything for me.

But this is Mom we're talking about here, and when she gets a hangnail, the world stops until we can find the nail clippers.

"I've heard that before," I said.

"Well, the two of you are going to have to do something for supper. I can't stand on my feet," said Mom.

Dad looked like a little kid who couldn't find his parents when he heard that. He likes to eat, and Mom is a great cook, but every once in awhile she'll come home and say, "Here, you cook tonight. I'm tired," and Dad will make something.

It's usually pretty awful. He made rice once that was

so gummy you could blow bubbles with it, and he made a roast beef dinner another time that was so bad Mom threw the whole thing out and cooked another one. We ate supper that night at eleven o'clock.

I walked over to the drawer where we have all of our take-out menus and opened it and said, "You wanna phone or do you want me to?"

Dad laughed at that. Even Mom started laughing and shaking her head.

"My men," she said. "What would you two do if I ever decided to go away somewhere?"

"Move in at Kelly's," I said. Kelly's is this restaurant in town that serves pretty good food. I like their chicken and Dad always gets their spaghetti, although I don't know why. Mom makes delicious spaghetti.

We decided to order a pizza, and when it came time to choosing the toppings, instead of fighting over pepperoni and mushroom versus The Kitchen Sink Combo, which has absolutely everything on it, including a little doughball in the center in the shape of a kitchen sink (that's the kind I like), we went with the pepperoni and mushroom.

Then I said to Mom, "You want me to get a salad, too?" and she just about fell off her chair, because normally, I turn greener than the lettuce when she brings a salad around. It's not because I don't like salad, it's just that when you're a doctor's son, and your mother is a health nut, you get things like salad and brown bread rammed down your throat so much you think you're going to choke. But this time I thought, if I'm going to be nice, I might as well go all the way with it.

So I ordered a salad.

The other thing I did was, I sat with them through the entire meal. I didn't eat a piece of pizza at the table, then pile a few on to a plate and hit the road to my bedroom. I didn't even turn the TV on in the living room so I could listen to it instead of them.

I sat through the entire meal, and finally when we were almost finished Dad said, "Is everything okay with you, Harper?" Obviously they were noticing a difference.

"With me? Yeah, I think so," I said, as if sitting there with them was something I did all the time.

Then Mom got into it.

"How are things at school?" she said.

"Same," I said, meaning not great. "I passed my math test the other day. I couldn't believe I passed it. It was that test on the two chapters that somebody ripped out of my book."

"Did you tell the principal about that?" said Dad. He got pretty ticked off when I told him what had happened. I don't know if he was mad because something happened to me, or because something is always happening to me, and it doesn't look good on him.

"I told my counsellor. There's not much point telling the principal. All he'd do is make an announcement and then everyone would know that I'd told him."

"How are things going with Ms. Davis?" Mom asked.

It was the first time she had ever asked me how things were going with Ms. Davis.

"Not bad," I said. Of course, I was thinking about

the note I had written at my writing class. I practically started shaking I was so nervous.

"Is she helping you at all?" Dad asked. He's one of these guys who doesn't really believe in counselling and all that (not that I do either, but I'm starting to come around a bit, I think). He thinks that if you have a healthy body, you should have a healthy mind, and if you don't have a healthy mind, then what you need to do is go for a jog or do some push-ups or something to clear your head.

"She told me I should start being nicer to you guys and you would start being nicer to me."

Wow. I said it and I didn't even know I was saying it. I didn't look them in the eye or anything either when I said it. I was looking at the dishes I was putting in the dishwasher. In fact, if you want to know the truth, I was staring so hard at those dishes, I thought they were going to crack.

Everything was silent for about a minute. I don't know what they were thinking, but my heart was pounding so loud I thought the neighbors were going to come over and ask me to turn it down.

"Is that what all this is about then?" said Mom. She had her "I'm-in-control" voice on.

"You mean supper and everything?"

"Yes."

"Sort of, I guess."

Of course, it was. Two years ago Mom had her arm in a sling for a week after she hurt her elbow, and I didn't even pour a glass of water for her. Mind you, she blamed me for hurting her elbow — it was my skateboard she stepped on that sent her flying.

"What have you been telling her about us?" said Mom.

"Not much, really. She just thinks I should start communicating more effectively with you guys (I love that phrase). She says it's one of the things I could write about in my essay."

"And what do you think?"

I started to say something but then I stopped. I couldn't get my mind off that stupid note I wrote. So I decided to give it to them. I went to my coat at the back door and dug my scribbler from the Cafe out of my pocket. Then I went over to them and handed it to Mom, but before I did, I told them what it was.

"See, I wrote this note at my writing class the other night. It's nothing really bad or anything, but I showed it to Ms. Davis, and she thought you should see it. That's what got us talking about how I'm feeling and everything."

Mom read the note and then passed it to Dad. Then she looked me right dead in the eye. I thought she was mad at first, but then these big tears started welling up and dropping down her cheeks. I don't see Mom cry very often. She never makes any noise or anything when she's doing it. She just cries a little, then blows her nose and the whole thing is done with.

"I feel empty sometimes, too," she said.

Well that got me going. I started blubbering and shaking like those people you see on the witness stand on TV.

Pretty soon we were both crying. I don't know what

97

Dad was doing. He's not the crying type. I'm not even sure if he knew what we were crying about.

After a minute or two, he got up and pulled a box of Kleenex from the counter behind me. I grabbed about six pieces and started honking away. Then Mom started and we ended up laughing. We sounded like a flock of geese flying south for the winter.

"Good thing Mr. Carson's not home. He'd probably run over here with his rifle and start shooting," I said. Mr. Carson is this neighbor of ours who goes hunting all the time and always tells us about it.

"I don't think he'd hit anything," said Dad, who didn't seem to mind my attempts at lightening the mood. "He never seems to come home with anything but a head cold."

Mom took awhile before she started talking. She dabbed all the tears out of her eyes and blew her nose about a thousand times. You could tell she was thinking.

"I never knew you could write so well," she said.

My Mom doesn't compliment people very often, except when they're in her store, where everyone over ten is beautiful and very wise, and everyone under ten is adorable and very bright, unless you're Martha Fishburn, this classmate of mine — if you can consider someone you sit beside everyday and never say a word to a classmate — who my mom thinks is just adorable, and who I think is about as bright as a Christmas bulb in mid-June.

"You think this is good?" I said. I know I wasn't exactly sticking to the subject of the evening, but I wasn't about to let a comment like that slip away untouched.

"Well, all I know about writing is, if you can touch a person's heart, it's good, and you have touched my heart with this note," said Mom.

It's funny, you know, but Mom is always telling me to look people in the eye when you talk with them, but when she said that she was looking at some speck or something on the kitchen table as hard as I was staring at those dishes.

"I didn't mean to," I said. I was kind of apologizing. I didn't want to make her cry.

"Harper," she said, lifting her head so her eyes were back on mine. "That was a compliment. You should say thank you when someone gives you a compliment. You accept it. You don't deny it. Believe me, they don't come along every day."

"Okay," I said. "Thank you."

"You're welcome," she said, and she smiled at me, and I could tell she was thinking that I was not such a lousy kid to spend time with after all, and I must admit, I was kind of thinking the same thing about her and Dad.

"Now let's get back to what you said."

twelve

I suppose I could go into a bunch of detail about what we talked about, but I'm going to be writing it up in my essay anyway, and anybody who wants to can see it there.

I learned a few things about my parents and we got into some of the things that were bothering me. When I told Mom I was mad at her the other night, she said, "Why didn't you say anything?"

"'Cause I was mad," I said.

"Well we're going to have to do something about that," she said.

When we started packing up for bed, Dad said, "So how does it feel to be nice for a night?" and I said, in my best fatherly voice, "Dad, it's something you'll have to find out for yourself." He thought that was pretty funny.

Mom gave me a hug before I went upstairs. It wasn't one of those nothing hugs you get sometimes from people. My brother's wife, for example, always looks like she wants to run her shirt down to the cleaners after she hugs me. And at Christmas, when everyone really gets loveable and starts kissing each other, she always gives me one of those dry little pecks on the cheek. Sometimes she doesn't even touch my cheek. She just leans forward and kisses the air in front of it. It's not that I'm a dirty person or anything. In our house, cleanliness has pulled even with Godliness in terms of importance. She just doesn't like me, for some reason.

Anyway, Mom gave me a real hug before I went to bed. She wrapped her arms around me so tightly that I felt like I was in the grip of an octopus. My face went flat up against her chest. I was stuck there and I couldn't move, but I really didn't mind it.

While she was holding me, she said, "You know, Harper, we have had some good times over the years," and I started thinking about some of the things I wrote about in class, and I said, "I know Mom. I want them to come back."

After about a minute she let me go and we looked at each other and sort of smiled. I could tell she was going to start crying again pretty soon, so I said good night and ran up to my room.

When I got there, I thought about all the things we had talked about, and I realized that for the first time in a long time, I actually felt that I belonged in my own home.

It was pretty weird. I almost started crying again myself.

thirteen

Ms. Davis was away on Monday, so I didn't get a chance to tell anyone about how things were going with my parents until class Tuesday night.

I walked in and Patty was there at her desk by the door, plugging in her Sony Walkman. I asked her what tape she was listening to. I already knew the answer, but I just felt like talking.

"Anne Murray," she said.

"Isn't she kind of old?" I said. My parents listen to Anne Murray.

"She drinks eight cups of water a day to stay healthy," said Patty.

"Wow. I bet she goes to the bathroom more times than that."

"Quiet. My tape's on."

Del was at our table at the front of the class. I walked up behind her and told her to cover her eyes.

"If this is a stick-up, I should warn you, my husband is six-foot-five and weighs two hundred and eighty-five pounds," she said.

I put a two-liter bottle of Coke in front of her and said, "Don't move or I'll belch."

She opened her eyes and said, "I can't drink that. I'm on a new diet. I bet my son ten bucks that I can lose ten pounds by Christmas."

"So start tomorrow," I said.

"Well, okay, but give me a little glass."

"You'll never guess what's gone on in my house since I was here last week," I said, handing her the same coffee cup she has used since the class started.

"Let me see. You've painted the ceilings and walls. You've wallpapered the windows. Your mother has made everyone matching pantsuits to wear to church. Your father has given up politics and has become a boy scout leader. Your sister-in-law lost her job and came begging to you to help her find a new one. Am I getting close?"

"We've been nice to each other for almost a week."

Del stopped moving with her coffee cup in mid-air and looked at me to see if I was joking. When she saw the smile on my face, she said, "I'm impressed."

"So am I," I said. "You should see it. It's pretty neat."

"So are you all running around holding hands or what?"

"No. Nothing like that. But it's different."

When Josh came in, he asked me how things were going and I told him.

"Good for you," he said. "That was a pretty brave thing you did, showing them that letter."

"I was scared. When I passed it to Mom, I didn't know if she was going to come at me with a knife or hug me to death."

"Well, you're still here," said Del. "Where'd she stab you?"

"I've started doing it at school, too," I said. "I saw my gym teacher the other day getting out of his car, and I walked by him and said, 'Hey, Mr. Jorgenson, nice car,' and he looked at me like I'd just swiped his hubcaps."

"Had you?" said Del.

"No, but when I walked by him, I said, 'Just giving you a compliment. They don't come by everyday, you know.' I'm sure he thought I was nuts."

"How's the essay coming?" said Josh.

He had to burst my bubble.

"I haven't started it yet," I said. It's due at the end of this week.

"You want a hand?"

"Sure," I said.

I thought he was going to sit down and help me write it, but instead he went to where he always stands when he's talking to the class and said, "Okay, tonight what I want you to do is, I want you to think of a time in your life when you were sad, or lonely, or angry at someone, and how you turned yourself around. What did you do? Did you talk to somebody? Did you go to church? Did you change anything about your own behavior? Did you take action? Tell me what you did."

That sent everyone off to work and I sat there and thought about what else I could write about aside from being nice, since, in reality, not even that was going to get me very far. I mean, Mom and Dad think it's alright, but my brother thinks I'm trying to hide something, and my sister thinks I just want to get out of writing the essay. In other words, being nice to them hasn't changed a thing.

And at school it's impossible to be nice to everybody. Darren Talbot pushed me out of the line at the cafeteria again. I was right there ready to get some soup and he came and told me the fire chief wanted to see me in the principal's office. All of his goony friends laughed, then they butted in and told me to get to the end of the line, so I decided to go to my locker instead and eat by myself.

Ms. Davis can say what she wants, but sometimes being distant is the only way to survive in that high school.

When our writing time was up everybody read their stories out loud. I started writing down some of the things they were saying because I figured that's what Josh wanted me to do, but then I started to get a feel for what was going on.

All of their stories were different. Lou wrote about why he burned the schoolhouse down. He said that when he was in grade four, his teacher used to start everyday by asking a student to pull a letter out of this giant box she had at the front of the class. Then she would ask the student to tell everyone what the letter was, and then say two words that began with it.

She called Lou one day and he went and did what he was told, except Lou didn't know anything about the alphabet, so he had no idea if he was holding a "B" or an "L" or what, and she got very upset with him and called him ignorant, which he didn't understand, and told him he was just like his father.

The thing was, Lou didn't even know who his father was, and didn't know a thing about him, but when the teacher said that, he got a picture in his head of a man standing at the front of a classroom with a bunch of kids laughing at him because he didn't know the alphabet.

It wasn't too long after that that all the kids had to go to the church for school because the schoolhouse was no longer available.

Debra told us about riding the bus with a bunch of school kids who kept calling her names all the time. She said one of them used to make her cry everyday until a friend of her mother's, who happens to be a policeman, gave her a tube of pepper spray to scare them off with. "Be careful if you ever use it," he said. "This stuff can really sting."

So the very next day, she got on the bus and the kid who always made her cry tried to pull her book bag off her shoulder, which was something he did almost all the time, but Debra was holding on to the strap of her bag very tightly, so when he yanked on it, he pulled her right to the floor of the bus.

Now usually when he did this, she would start to cry and the bus driver would pull over and warn everybody, but this time, she reached into her book bag, pulled out the pepper spray, and let the guy have it right between the eyes.

"He never rode the bus again," said Debra. "And the next time I saw him, he crossed the street and ran home."

Billy told us about the time he went to a drama club to learn more about acting, and they made him pretend he was a tree all night. This was the story I liked the best.

"They thought I was joking," he said.

"Why did they think you were joking?" asked Debra.

"I told them I wanted to be a Klingon on 'Star Trek' and they didn't believe me."

Anyway, because he refused to leave, they told him to stand in the corner all night with his arms over his head. According to Billy, his arms got so tired, somebody had to chop him down.

When he showed up at the next class, they told him to do the same thing. When he showed up at the next class, they asked him what he was doing, so he told them again that he wanted to be an actor, and they told him that he was becoming a bit of a nuisance, and suggested that he find somewhere else to hang out.

So Billy went home and wrote a letter to this person he had written several letters to in the past several years, and this person, who had told Billy to enroll in an acting class if he was serious about becoming an actor, wrote back to Billy and said, "If they don't take you into their acting class, I will personally come down and find out what the problem is."

So Billy took the letter with him to the next acting class and showed the instructor, and the instructor laughed and threw it in the garbage.

So then Billy wrote another letter to this person, who happened to be William Shatner of "Star Trek," except Billy kept on calling him "Captain Kirk," even in his letters, and told him everything that had happened, and gave him the name and address of the acting class, and a list of the buses that went through that part of the city, in case "The Captain" ran into difficulty getting there, and waited very eagerly for the reply.

But he never got one. He waited for a few weeks because it usually took at least a month to get a letter back, but nothing came in the mail. He left his answering machine on whenever he went outside, but he never received a call.

Then one day, about six months later, Billy was walking in front of the theater where the acting class was held, and he walked straight into the head instructor who grabbed Billy by the shoulders, gave him a great big hug, and led him inside to his office.

On his wall in a frame was a letter that said, "If you are absolutely, one-hundred-percent sure that this young man cannot become an actor, then you better think again. Sincerely, William Shatner."

I guess the instructor had done everything he could to get a hold of Billy, but because Billy had never left his name, telephone number, or address, the guy couldn't really do too much. But from that day on, Billy has been going to the acting classes.

Del wrote about a parenting group she joined when she had her first baby, and how out-of-place everyone made her feel because she was an unwed, teenage mother. So she took home all of these books on parenting from the local library, and when her daughter was asleep she read them, and after about two months, the only person who could answer Del's questions was the group's instructor, and after about six months, Del was running a little group of her own, and by the time her daughter turned two, Del was putting on a series of workshops on single parenting and hosting a support group for pregnant teenagers.

I didn't read mine because I didn't write anything, but Mom was a few minutes late picking me up, so I had a chance to write a few things down.

Before I left, Josh said that he would be in on Friday if I wanted him to take a look at my essay. I didn't know for sure if I wanted him to or not, but I said okay anyway. I asked if he had any tips for me.

"Just write what you feel," he said. "Leave yourself some time to read it over when you're done, and think about what you're going to say, but when you start writing, don't worry about format or anything like that. Just go with it. That's when you do best."

He told me a few other things, then I said good-bye and went downstairs. I felt like I was going to war or something. Everybody was wishing me luck and giving me advice. Billy asked if I needed to borrow his pencil sharpener.

Debra asked if I would be coming back after my essay was finished. I said probably. She said, "Good. I like it when you're here."

It's nice hearing things like that sometimes.

fourteen

I went and saw Ms. Davis the next morning and showed her my notes and told her what I was going to say in my essay. It's not like I had everything mapped out or anything like that, but some things were starting to come clear to me. I still wanted her to see what I had, though. They weren't that clear.

She made some suggestions and helped me with a few of my ideas. I think we both understand each other a bit better now. I know I understand her better.

Before I left, I asked if she thought I was on the right track.

"Oh, I think so," she said. "I think you've done some real thinking about this. I'm excited to see that. I'm excited to see the essay." She meant it, too. That was one of the things about Ms. Davis. She meant everything she said. Not everybody in my life is like that.

"I'm excited to see it, too," I said.

"So when do you think you're going to write it?"

"Tonight. Then I can read it tomorrow night and give it to him on Friday."

She looked at me and smiled again and for a minute or so, I got the feeling she was going to say something big and profound, like, You've come a long way, Harper, or something like that, but instead she just said, "Good luck with it," and left it at that.

"Thanks," I said, and left her office.

I wish someone had wished me all of this luck before I got into this mess. I wouldn't even be here.

fifteen

I stayed up all night and finished the thing at five-thirty this morning. Mom told me to stay in bed and enjoy the day, which sounded just fine to me.

You can read it, but promise you won't laugh, and if you have any suggestions, save them. You might need them for your own some day.

Here it is.

HOW I PLAN TO TURN MY LIFE AROUND
by Harper Winslow

Your Honor,

I am not the greatest essay writer in the world, so please bear with me. The other thing is, I'm pretty nervous, so if you see a word that doesn't look right somewhere, it's probably because I hit the wrong key by accident. I'm normally a pretty good speller.

Anyway, here it is. I hope you like it. I put a lot of thought into it, like you said I should. I don't know how a person could write an essay like this without putting a lot of thought into it.

My counsellor at school, her name is Ms. Davis, said I should go with my own words instead of her fancy phrases, but just so you know that I know them, here are a few of the things she said I could do that would help me turn my life around.

The first is to communicate more effectively with my parents, and other important people in my life, like teachers. I have tried this with my mom and dad and it's worked pretty well so far.

We had a long talk about two weeks ago. I showed them this letter I had written about how lonely I was feeling. That got them going. They told me all about what it was like when I was born. Mom said she was really busy with her store, and Dad was starting his own medical clinic. My brother and sister were into their teens and doing crazy things like staying out after their curfew and refusing to make their beds. Not exactly the stuff you'd turn into a movie, but Mom and Dad said it was very stressful and when Mom found out she was pregnant, well, you could just imagine.

None of this meant much to me. Maybe it should have, but it didn't, so I said to them, "I thought we were talking about me tonight."

Well, Mom got a bit steamed over that comment, but, because we were being nice to each other, she never said anything. She just smiled and said, "Okay, honey, let's talk about you."

So we talked about me for the rest of the time and Dad didn't yawn even once! He even said at one point,

"You're a bright kid, you know that?" I said, "Thanks Dad. You're pretty bright yourself."

He doesn't mind it when I get like that with him. At least, not when he's in a good mood. He said he misses it, actually. Mom said that's because Dad was the smart alec of his family, so that's who I got it from.

We talked about a lot of things that night. I told them that I hate the way they're always getting tutors for me without asking what the problem is. Mom said, "How can we ask you anything when you're always up in your room?" So I said, "Well you're never home, so what am I supposed to do?"

You can see what kinds of things we have to work out, but Ms. Davis said that now that the issues are out in the open, they will be easier to deal with.

She also asked me what my goals are. She asked me this the meeting after I told her about this dog that I've always wanted but have never been allowed to have because I wasn't responsible enough.

I got pretty upset the day I told her about it, so the next time I went to see her, she asked me to think about what I would have to do to get my own dog. Then she brought up this idea of goal setting. She said we could start with a a basic one like getting to school on time and work our way up from there.

It took me a few weeks to warm to the idea, but now I have a little list of a few things I want to do. Getting a dog is one of them. I have to talk to Mom and Dad about what I have to do to get one.

I'm sure they're going to make me do the dishes

*and shovel the sidewalk and do better at school, but I
would really like a dog.*

*We also talked about setting aside one day of every
month to be a Family Day, although I don't know if
that is possible or not. Dad says he is so busy these
days, he has to check in his daytimer to find out when
he can come home. So we may have to settle for a
Family Hour or something, for starters anyway.*

*At school, I'm going to sign up for the newspaper.
I have been doing a lot of writing lately, and I've
discovered that I really enjoy it. I mean, I used to
write all the time, but I never showed anyone, but
since I joined this writing class, I've discovered that I
am actually pretty good at it (at least, that's what my
instructor says), and Ms. Davis has been encouraging
me since I first saw her to get more involved at school.*

*Those are the two main things that I talked about
with her, communication and goal-setting. Everything
else that I learned about turning my life around came
from the writing class Mom put me in.*

*It is called The Tuesday Cafe. The people in it are
not at all what you would expect. They sure weren't
what I was expecting. They are all learning how to
read and write. Some of them are mentally handicapped.*

*I know what you think I'm going to say is, "Now I
know how thankful I should be because these people
are handicapped and I'm not, and some of them have
been disadvantaged right from the start, while I
haven't been, so maybe I should stop complaining and*

just get on with my life."

Well, that's true, to a point, but Ms. Davis said that the frustration I felt the day I started that fire was real, and the loneliness I feel is real, and that to tell myself to stop crying and be happy would be, in her words, "negating my inner pain."

I think I know what she means by that.

Anyway, at one of my meetings with her, she asked me to think about why I have such a hard time getting along with other people, and no problem at all getting along with the people in my writing class.

I didn't know the answer at first, but at the last class I went to my friend Del basically gave it to me. I had been worrying about this essay and exactly what I was going to say in it, and she said, "Just show him who you are. That will be good enough. He'll like that." Then I realized that this was the first class I have ever been to where I didn't try to separate myself from everyone else.

Usually I sit in the back of the room at school. I don't talk to anyone. When we have to do something in pairs, I'll just sit and wait for everyone else to get their partner, then I'll go with the odd man out. That's just the way it has always been for me at school. I've never really seemed to click with anyone.

But at this place, I sat right at the front of the class because Del was serving me Coca-Cola for the whole two hours, and no one ever asked me who I was or where I lived or what my parents did. They didn't judge me or anything like that, and I guess I didn't *judge them. They just started talking to me like I was a human being, and I just talked back to them, as if they were, too.*

It's kind of funny, actually, but it was the last place I thought of looking for a friend, and the only place I've ever found one.

Anyway, at the last class, the instructor, his name is Josh, asked everyone to write a story about a time when they were unhappy or lonely in their lives and how they got to be happy again.

They all had lots of stories to tell, and as I listened to them, I began to see something. I told Ms. Davis and she helped me figure out what it is.

This is what we came up with.

I used to think that I would never get along with my parents and that I would never have any friends.

I used to see Mom and Dad getting all dressed up to go out for dinner or a party, and they still sit around the table after supper some nights and go over the various invitations they've received, and decide which ones they can accept and which ones they'd rather not go to, or couldn't go to, and I could never in a million years picture myself doing the same thing, because I have never had an invitation to a party, much less two on the same night.

I remember sometimes lying in bed and listening to my brother and sister laugh it up with Mom and Dad, and I can see with my own eyes how excited Mom gets whenever my brother brings his family around, or when my sister brings hers around, and I would try to see Mom getting excited over me coming home, but I never really could.

I think this is why I got so frustrated.

Then I listened to all of these stories by the people in my class and I started to realize that life changes for people, and I can control how it will change for me.

I mean, this one woman, Susan, she's really, really skinny, and one day I asked her why she doesn't eat more, and she told me this story about when she was eleven, her mom died, so she was moved into a boarding house, and the woman who ran the place hated to cook, and was a lousy cook, but she always made Susan eat everything she made, even if it was completely burned or totally raw in the middle, and Susan used to get sick every night, and now she hated food.

Anyway, Susan told us a story about when she was nine years old, she used to ride her bike around this little park at the end of her street and how this group of kids used to tease her because she still had training wheels on her bicycle.

She used to cry all the time, but her mom still made her go outside because the fresh air and exercise would be good for her.

The way it used to go was, these kids would be sitting in one of the shelters in the park smoking cigarettes and when they heard Susan come around, they would run outside and over this little hill and down to the bike path.

They could hear Susan coming because she had one of those little clickers on the spokes of her bike that would let people on the path know she was behind them. She liked the clicker on the spokes more than a bell because she had to take one of her hands off the handle bars to ring the bell, and she didn't like doing that.

So at the start of one of her rides one day, she decided to take the clicker off. She said she didn't know where the idea came from, but she did it, and she rode all around the park without making any noise, and the kids never came out of the shelter. In fact, they never bothered her again.

Now she has two friends she goes bike riding with, and whenever she sees kids with a clicker on the spokes of their bikes, she makes a point of saying hi to them so they won't feel bad.

So my point is, I can do things to deal with my unhappiness just like she did with hers. I mean, I know some things are going to happen whether I want them to or not, and, as Ms. Davis said, some people are just plain mean, no matter what you say to them, but they will not be in my life forever, and my life will go on and I have a say in where it's going.

I mean, I know I don't have a clicker I can take off my bike, but for the first time in my life I smiled at this girl I know, Martha Fishburn, and she smiled back at me. And I was nice to my parents for one whole night, and we've been pretty nice to each other ever since, although sometimes it's a good thing that they're not around very much.

I hope all of this makes sense.

Anyway, that's pretty much all I have to say. I think I'm at about 2,000 words, but I'm not completely sure.

Like I said, this might not be the greatest essay in the world, but I hope it's alright.

The other thing that Ms. Davis said to me was that if I really want to turn things around, I'll stay out of your courtroom. I think she might have something there.

sixteen

I took the essay in to Josh and he read it over and told me not to change anything. He said he thought it was fine just the way it is.

I had to hurry to get it to the courthouse on time, but I wanted to ask him something first. I wanted to know if the message I got about having control of my life was the one he wanted me to get, and he said, "You never know what you'll learn when you leave your ears open."

I want to remember that.

I told him I would be returning on Tuesday for another class. He said he was looking forward to seeing me again and congratulated me on a job well done.

My parents said they thought my essay was terrific.

Lately I've been getting the feeling that my life has been turning for me ever since I stepped out of that courtroom, I just didn't know it until now.

Maybe I'm wrong, but I don't think so.

Anyway, I have to run. Today I find out what kind of community service work I have to do.

What a thrill that's going to be.